TOM MEETS THE UNKNOWN

A hand fell on his shoulder. Tom spun around with his cudgel raised high.

His mother dropped back in alarm.

"Tom, lad! Get a hold of yourself. What is it? Who was out there?"

Tom lowered his stick. "Forgive me, Mother. It was horrible. It was —"

Somehow, the admission he had been about to make refused to pass his lips. How could he say it was himself who had stood out there, and broken the serenity of their night? It seemed shameful somehow, criminal and illicit, that he had confronted his double. It was as if some secret part of himself wanted nothing more than an end to their peaceful existence, and had contrived this disturbance expressly for that very purpose.

Tom's mother looked on expectantly. "Yes, Tom, go on. What was it?"

Tom told half the truth. "It was — a boggle. A horrid boggle, the likes of which I've never seen. One great staring eye, no mouth, a single hand and foot. It seemed ready to jump in, when I slammed the door upon it. I think it's gone now," he added hopefully.

Harp, Pipe, & Symphony

Paul Di Filippo

COSMOS BOOKS

HARP, PIPE, & SYMPHONY

Published by
Dorchester Publishing Co., Inc.
200 Madison Ave.
New York, NY 10016
in collaboration with Wildside Press LLC

ISBN-10: 0-8439-6070-1
ISBN-13: 978-0-8439-6070-9

Printed in the United States of America.

TO DEBORAH
Prettier than Queen Mab
and far less capricious.

"The tale is not beautiful if nothing is added to it."

—Tuscan proverb, quoted by Italo Calvino
in *Italian Folktales*

"Allegory, if its persons have life, is a prostitution of their personalities, forcing them for an end other than their own . . . To me, the persons are the argument."

—E. R. Eddison, *The Mezentian Gate*

"*Heere is the queene of Fayerye,*
With harpe and pipe and symphone,
Dwellynge in this place."

—Geoffrey Chaucer,
"The Tale of Sir Topaz"

Book 1

I

The Unexpected Luck of Widows' Sons

> "Gandalf, Gandalf! . . . Not the fellow who used to tell such wonderful tales at parties, about dragons and goblins and giants and the rescue of princesses and the unexpected luck of widows' sons?"
>
> — J. R. R. Tolkien, *The Hobbit*

There came a knocking one moonless night at the door of the lonely cottage on the edge of the forest.

Thomas Rhymer, closing his book (one of two in the Rhymer house) upon his forefinger to mark his place, looked up at his mother. Sitting across the room in a chair fashioned of split logs, she had been knitting with the oily wool shorn from their own sheep, and spun on the big wheel that occupied one corner of the crowded cottage. Hearing the unexpected knock, she had dropped her wooden needles and the unfinished garment into her lap. Mixed candle- and fire-light danced upon her startled features, and Tom was reminded of the play of sunlight on wind-tossed autumn leaves. For a brief, disorienting moment, he was unsure whether the candle flame truly flickered in the drafts that criss-crossed the room, or whether the light was stable and her features writhed.

His mother's accustomed voice soon broke the unaccountable spell. Its familiarity restored somewhat the placid contentment Tom had been enjoying till that moment, immersed in his book.

"Whoever could that be, Tom," she asked, "abroad on such a night, with a storm coming on? Shall I answer, or will you?"

"Rest yourself, Mother," Tom said. "I'll attend to it. It's probably some traveller strayed from the Great Road to Ercildoune, in search of a night's lodging."

Tom stood, setting his book down upon the cane-bottomed chair, and his mother resumed her knitting, needles clicking like the fingers of a skeleton twiddling its thumbs. High above the thatched roof, thunder rumbled distantly in the heavens, portending heavy spring rain.

Moving toward the door, Tom considered who — or what — might be standing outside on their front step. Although he had minimized the untimely interruption to his mother, he didn't care for it at all. A vague premonition, almost like a memory displaced from his own future, seemed to warn him against opening the door, as if to do so would be to insure that nothing would ever again be the same.

Tom sought to shake himself out of the queer mood. Surely it was nothing more than a reaction to the odd flight of fancy he had had a moment ago, when it looked as if the long-known and comforting face of his mother was melting like that of a waxen dummy.

By the door, Tom lifted his knobby, well-polished walking stick — a stout length of hawthorn — from its resting place. No sense being unprepared. He was grateful that the door, opening inward and to his left, would block his mother's view of their late-night visitor.

The knock sounded again, not three inches from Tom's ear, peremptory and urgent, as if the unknown intruder, with a vital mission to accomplish, raced against an inexorable deadline.

Tom raised the thick wooden pin on its leather cord from the eye of the iron hasp. He swung aside the hinged and slatted portion of the latch that fitted over the staple set into the door itself. He set his hand upon the smooth handle and prepared to pull the door open.

A loud whiplike CRACK! sounded from behind him, like the Devil's lash snapping at his tailbone. Tom jumped a foot, heart thudding high in his throat, where no heart ever belonged.

But it was only a dry branch succumbing to the flames in the stone hearth.

His traitorous heart gradually sank back into his chest. A pain in his right hand made him realize he was clutching his walking stick as if it were a root protruding from a cliff down which he hung. Loosening his grip a trifle, he again turned to the door.

A third time the knock sounded, urging haste.

Breathing deeply, Tom pulled open the door.

The angled mass of broad planks blocked the interior illumination behind Tom. The night seemed to extend a hungry tongue of darkness into the room, lapping at all that had seemed secure and inviolate. Thunder spoke throatily, like a giant requesting entrance.

Tom could see nothing clearly at first, his eyes used to the light. There seemed to be a single, man-sized shape on the step.

Silently cursing his stupidity in not carrying a candle, Tom opened his mouth to speak.

Lightning scribed itself across the sky, a hieroglyph of unreadable significance. In the second of the lightning's brief electric reign, Tom saw who awaited him.

It was himself.

But a self he had never been.

Haggard, unshaven (save for a bald patch on the figure's left jaw), hollow-cheeked, uncouth clothes in tatters, Tom's doppleganger stood mutely upon the uneven stone serving as the cottage's front step. Staring deliberately into Tom's eyes, the apparition appeared content merely to survey his double. It neither beckoned nor spoke nor moved, but only studied Tom as if he were an object of immense wonder, perhaps a precious idol from some faraway empire, or some new species of mankind.

Tom was transfixed. For that infinitesimal, yet infinite moment during which the lightning blazed, he could neither move nor think. Had someone trodden upon his foot or poked him with a pitchfork, he would have remained as paralyzed as before.

And then the incandescent crack in the night sky was gone, and Tom was released. Uttering a high-pitched shout, he took a step back. Thunder spoke again, hard upon the lightning. Tom fumbled for the edge of the door, intending to slam it shut.

White fire split the sky once more, like an axe cleaving a swollen fruit.

Dazed and frightened, Tom had a confused and jumbled second to see that something had joined his double upon the step.

One eye, one hand, one foot, a ruff of hair like a wire brush —

No, impossible, there were no such things.

Tom's frantic hand found the edge of the door. As he swung it with all his strength, he heard his double speak, in Tom's own voice.

"Damn it all, Lug! I told you to stay back! Now you've spoiled everything!"

The door filled its frame with a loud crash, and Tom leaped upon it to secure it.

One cheek pressed against the rough planks, breathing as if he had just run a race, Tom waited fearfully for his double to resume pounding on the door. Seconds passed. There was no noise beyond the reassuringly thick barricade except the soughing of wind and the mumble of thunder.

A hand fell on his shoulder. Tom spun around with his cudgel raised high.

His mother dropped back in alarm.

"Tom, lad! Get a hold of yourself. What is it? Who was out there?"

Tom lowered his stick. "Forgive me, Mother. It was horrible. It was —"

Somehow, the admission he had been about to make refused to pass his lips. How could he say it was himself who had stood out there, and broken the serenity of their night? It seemed shameful somehow, criminal and illicit, that he had confronted his double. It was as if some secret part of himself wanted nothing more than an end to their peaceful existence, and had contrived this disturbance expressly for that very purpose.

Tom's mother looked on expectantly. "Yes, Tom, go on. What was it?"

Tom told half the truth. "It was — a boggle. A horrid boggle, the likes of which I've never seen. One great staring eye, no mouth, a single hand and foot. It seemed ready to jump in, when I slammed the door upon it. I think it's gone now," he added hopefully.

Tom's mother regarded him with concern and sympathy. The wrinkles around her grey eyes — all the Learmonts were famous for their eyes the color of a choppy sea on a cloudy day — seemed to penetrate beneath the facade of his story to the true source of his anxiety. Gently, she said, "Tom, perhaps it's that book. Do you really think such fancies are good to dwell upon?"

"There's naught wrong with the work of Master Alighieri, Mother," Tom protested, recalling a bit guiltily the nervous excitement the much-handled, leather-bound book was capable of engendering in him. "It's a good, pious tale, with no harm in it. And you must admit, Mother, no reading of mine could have conjured up those three knocks."

"Still —" His mother's voice trailed off, unwilling to push the point.

Tom was beginning to recover his usual cheerfulness. "Let's forget the whole incident, Mother. Real boggle or imagined, it's gone now. Let's call this night at an end. We've plenty of work to do tomorrow."

Before his mother could prolong the conversation further, Tom turned away and began puttering about the immaculate room as if to set things right before retiring.

He wound the loudly ticking clock that sat upon the mantlepiece like a minor and somewhat simpleminded godling. Spotting his splayed-open book upon his chair, he carefully picked it up, closed it and placed it on its accustomed shelf. Then he swept a few stray cinders from the hearth with a broom made of straw bound onto the end of a gnarly stick. He swooped down on a stray mug that had been left upon the supper table, rinsed it in a bucket of water and hung it from a hook beside its mates. A cobweb shifting wispily in a draft caught his glance, and with the broom he brought it down from the shadow-filled rafters.

Finally, when even his ingenious eye could find no more excuses to avoid bidding his mother goodnight, he turned toward where he knew she would be sitting.

In the southern wall of the house — the warmest, both because of the direction of prevailing winds, and the proximity of a stand of trees outside — there were two sets of double-doors, embellished with carvings of flowers and leaves. These doors were of a curious sort. Their lower edges began about two feet off the floor, and their tops ended a mere three feet above that. In width, they were about four feet. Anyone contemplating a hasty exit through them would have received an abrupt surprise, since they opened onto deep sleeping alcoves, filled with corn-shuck mattresses and thick quilts.

Tom's mother sat on the sill of her bed. She had let down her white-streaked hair, and it flowed over the shoulders of her blue flannel gown like soot-peppered snow.

"Tom," she said tentatively, "I know it's not the same with me as with your father, but if ever you want to talk —"

Tom shook his head no.

His mother sighed. "Goodnight then, Tom. You're a good son. See you in the morning."

Pulling her legs up into her bed and closing the doors, Tom's mother retired for the night.

Snuffing out the last lit candle, Tom did the same.

In his shuttered cabinet-bed, Tom clumsily shucked off his outer shirt and pants, retaining his linen undershirt and woolen trews for warmth. Under the musty comforters, he could feel his body-heat seeping out and filling the alcove. Even now, in early April, the nights were cold and the blankets welcome.

Tom waited for sleep to come. After an indeterminate time, he knew that Morpheus must have forgotten the appointment. His brain felt like a churn in which the milk of experience was being painfully transformed into the butter of wisdom. It seemed as if his entire life — and especially the confusing events just past — were filing by in a contorted, out-of-sequence review, from which he had to extract the sense.

Thunder punctuated his uneasy reverie.

The book he had been reading was part of the key. That infernal, glorious, purging book! What had motivated that mad Italian to write it? What were those "dark woods" he had been lost in? Was the whole extravagant journey just a gloss on that forbidding masterwork, the Bible (the other book in the Rhymer household), or was it actually a subversive undermining of orthodoxy?

The answer, he had once thought, lay in Purgatory.

Tom was familiar with Purgatory, of course, from interminable sermons given each Sunday by the fat village priest in the echoing, musty, stone church not far from the Rhymer house. But the priest's vague descriptions of Purgatory had only piqued Tom's curiosity regarding this queer half-way station between Heaven and Hell. In the rigid scheme of good and evil — which at times felt like a tight strap around Tom's forehead — Purgatory seemed like a possible token of some middle way between two equally tedious extremes.

Through all the years of his young maturity, Tom had been puzzled by the dualism of life, as filtered through the teachings of his church and society in general. Why — if his mentors were right — was there such a consistent, unbreachable dichotomy in life? Saints and sinners, the saved and the damned, right and wrong, good and bad, Heaven and Hell, charity and greed, the meek and the aggressors — the whole catalogue of opposites that were preached at him every Sunday, and implemented — even if only halfheartedly — by everyone the rest of the week. It seemed wrong to Tom that in every sphere of action, mankind had but two choices. His instinctive reading of the world was more complex than that. There seemed to be an infinity of choices at every crisis point, any number of ways one could respond, none of which was strictly labeled in the way he had been taught.

When Master Alighieri's book had come into his hands, he had devoured it eagerly, intuitively sensing from the outset that it might hold an answer to his questions, perhaps even the truth about good and evil.

At first, reading the section called *Purgatorio*, Tom thought he had come upon that bright middle way he sought, between the iron-bound choice of Heaven or

Hell. In the earthly histories of those spirits whom Alighieri depicted as deserving of partial redemption — or at least of respite from damnation — Tom thought to find a model for his own behavior, one which would hew neither to traditional virtue nor vice. The notion had proved barren, however. The inhabitants of Purgatory had turned out to be nothing more than conventionally noble heathens.

And of their "happy" fate, Tom wasn't so sure anymore, either.

The more he read, the more he regarded Purgatory as simply the attenuated borderlands of the infernal domain, where torture was not absent, but only subtle, consisting of eternal languishment, with nothing to turn one's strengths to and no hope of reprieve. This was not what he dimly envisioned as the bright and glorious kingdom awaiting all those who forged a perilous, exhilarating path between the conventional extremes.

No, this book — vivid, exciting, masterful as it might be — did not contain the key to the riddle of his life.

From the book, his thoughts naturally turned to the one who had given it to him.

His father.

Harl Rhymer had seemed a very old man when Tom was young. Now, Tom knew he had been in his early sixties when Tom was born. (Tom's mother had reached that decade only recently.) But during his childhood, the man had seemed as ancient as the tall, secretive oaks that brooded at the cottage's back. Working in the fields or tending their small flock of sheep, Tom and his father had been an unlikely pair. The son was thin, fast and wiry; the father slow, bullish and deliberate.

All day Tom would chatter a hundred questions, which his father would answer with a monosyllable or, at most, a short phrase. Somehow the inconclusive answers, which had once placated Tom, seemed totally inadequate now.

Hoeing a row of corn, Tom would ask, "Father, what is truth?"

Without looking up from his work, Harl would reply, "A figment."

Tom would nod and consider the answer for a time. Then he might say, "Father, why are there hundreds of kinds of birds and fish, yet only two kinds of men, good and evil?"

"You are comparing things that have nothing in common. I cannot answer."

Tom found this unsatisfactory, but restrained himself from pursuing the matter. He had plenty of other questions in reserve.

So their days afield would pass, a parade of "whys and wherefores," followed by "becauses and therefores."

Occasionally, as Tom grew older, he would catch his father watching him circumspectly, with vast bemusement, as if marvelling at this inexplicable offspring of his old age. Despite his taciturn nature, Harl made a good listener, and Tom never hesitated to use him as a sounding-board for his dreams, ambitions and wild theories.

One day several years ago, his father had returned from the town of Ercildoune with a present for Tom. As if in wordless answer to all the questions he had been unable to banish over the years, he had handed Tom the book he had bartered for. Tom had regarded his father with new wonder, amazed that he had ever thought to provide such an unexpected supplement to his own small stock of answers.

Tom's effusive thanks had clearly embarrassed his father, who eventually turned away with hands raised in self-deprecation.

It was not long after that Harl had been unable to rise from bed one morning. Man of few words to the end of his life, he had been unable to pinpoint exactly what was wrong with him, save for a general listlessness and malaise. It was almost as if he felt his son had finally been fully provided for, and now his constant duties could be gratefully laid down. Tended assiduously by wife and son, Harl drifted comfortably into a death that seemed a natural extension of sleep. His final words had been plain: the names of his wife and son:

"Nora . . . Tom . . ."

The funeral party consisted of Tom, his mother, and her brother, Ross Learmont, who lived nearby on his own steading. In the kirkyard, a colorless sky wept fitfully, and the words of the priest went unheard by the family. Tom noticed tears in his uncle's grey eyes for the first time he could recall.

Weighed down by his covers, a draft tickling one exposed ear, Tom turned sleeplessly, helplessly following the tangled thread of his thoughts.

His father's face, fixed at one particular moment when Tom had caught him mysteriously contemplating his son, hovered in Tom's sight. Without warning, it suddenly wavered and melted into the face of Tom's doppleganger, as when that strange being had stood upon the step, regarding him with fervid intensity.

Do I really look like that? Tom wondered. The short, stiff black hair, the Learmont slate eyes, those quirked lips and aggressive rounded chin? Surely the supernatural thing that had been impersonating him had botched the imitation. And what could have been its motive for appearing so disheveled and wan? If it had intended to murder him and replace him, like some crib-snatched changeling, then why had it not duplicated him exactly? And what had been the nature and purpose of that improbable companion, so hastily glimpsed?

With these puzzles and others drifting in and out of focus, Tom gradually fell into a troubled sleep.

A thunder that wasn't awoke him. He sat up, groggy and uncertain of his whereabouts. The thunder rolled on and on, increasing in volume, unnatural in its timbre and failure to fade away.

With a start, he realized at last what he was hearing.

Hoofbeats.

A lot.

Suddenly, the shuttered box he had been sleeping in felt like a coffin covered with six feet of damp earth. He imagined he was suffocating, and might at any moment lose consciousness. Frantically, he kicked out, shoving aside the covers and bursting open the doors with a *bang*. Boosting himself forward and out, he whacked his head on the low overhang and saw alien constellations in red and black. His bare feet slapped the cold planks of the floor, sending a chill up his spine.

The ponderous drumroll of pounding hooves swelled portentously in his ears.

"Mother!" Tom shouted. "Get up! Quick! Something's happening!"

The doors of his mother's alcove began to swing aside, all too slowly. Tom yanked them open, and hustled Nora Rhymer out. In the dim light cast by the few red embers in the fireplace, Tom could see a dawning look of comprehension on her shadowed face, as the ominous sound penetrated her sleepiness.

Tom tried to project a confidence and competence he didn't feel. "It's probably nothing serious, Mother. But I think we'd best leave the house. Better to jump at a shadow than sit still for a boggle, as Uncle always says."

Tom tried to laugh, but only brought forth a nervous croak.

His mother nodded in agreement, and Tom raced through the cottage, gathering their shoes, two outer capes and, at the last minute, his prized book from its shelf and his walking stick from its sentry position by the door. Finally, the two of them rushed out the door, around one corner of the building, and a little ways into the sheltering woods.

The whole escapade — from awakening in a cozy bed to treading wet leaves under a canopy of dripping branches — had taken only a little over a minute. To Tom, the time had stretched like a soggy knitted scarf, sagging under the weight of the confusing events. He was reminded of how he and his double had seemed to stand frozen in mutual amazement for hours, although that too had been only seconds.

Time and the world seemed disordered tonight, deracinated and adrift.

It had begun to drizzle, and the air was chilly. Tom helped his mother don her shoes and cape, then put on his own. Together, they turned back toward the clearing that held the small manger that housed their flock, and the low-roofed cottage that had sheltered them for all Tom's life.

They had unintentionally ended up in the woods at a spot directly across the open yard from the path that lead out of their clearing and across their newly planted acres, merging thereafter with the Great Road. It was down this trail that they knew any riders would be coming.

With moisture trickling down the necks of their cloaks, they peered with mixed dread and hope from their concealment.

First appeared torchlight.

Bloody scarlet radiance flamed along the overarching limbs of the trees lining the path. The branches seemed to be consumed with a supernal fire that neither waxed nor abated.

Seconds behind the torchlight came the riders.

Two abreast, the hooves of their steeds chewing up great loamy divots, they careered up the trail like a precision troupe from some infernal circus. The sound of their headlong passage was like the sundering of the earth.

The lead duo split left and right upon entering the yard, and followed the outline of the cleared ground. Those behind them did the same, so that the periphery of the Rhymer property was soon sealed off by a picket of mounted men.

Under cover of the confusion, Tom dragged his mother back into the woods some distance further. They stopped where they could still spy on the fire-lit intruders. Tom couldn't bear to flee entirely — although he knew he could offer no resistance to these men — and his mother seemed paralyzed, without volition, by default consenting to Tom's dubious actions.

Now there was silence, save for the dripping of rain from leaves. The invaders seemed to be awaiting something, sitting like statues in a circle. Tom took advantage of the pause to study the nearest ones.

The men were clad in laquered red armor, like giant scarabs. They wore their plumed casques closed, hiding any trace of their faces. Those who did not bear torches carried long, wicked lances with elaborate blades like razor-sharp *fleurs-de-lys*. All had longswords scabbarded low on their hips.

Their caparisoned horses, Tom realized, were all chestnut bays, more red than brown, like creatures crusted with dried blood. The beasts were more impatient than their masters, pawing with barely restrained fury at the sodden earth and snorting in steamy puffs.

Movement at the gap in the ring where the path debouched caught Tom's attention. Someone new was entering.

The point man of this part of the procession was the pennant-bearer. On the end of a long pole, the damp gonfalon hung wetly, twisting in the rising storm-winds. As the man cantered into the center of the circle, Tom could make out the emblem sewn on the crimson standard.

It was a green lizard rampant, its tongue extended, its clawed digits raking at some unpictured foe.

Behind this figure rode several men in even more elaborate armor than the rest. Somehow they projected the air of courtiers, despite their military garb.

Last to enter was the most imposing figure of all.

A giant in his articulated iron suit, he rode a horse twice as big as any Tom had ever seen before tonight. The faceplate of his helmet was raised, revealing a shaven face as contorted as frost-heaved earth packed with stones and laced with roots.

He came to a stop at the center of his men. Again silence reigned. A tense expectancy filled the air.

The leader spoke.

His voice was flint and steel, wormwood and aconite.

"Bring me those who used to live here.

"Slaughter their cattle.

"Raze the last standing stick.

"Prepare a feast."

Tom's mother began to utter a sickened wail. Tom clamped a hasty hand on her mouth. Urgently he shuffled her deeper into the forest.

From the clearing, Tom heard a soldier call, "Your Illegitimacy, we find no inhabitants."

A titanic bellow of rage seemed to cause the trees themselves to cringe.

"We'll see if they think to hide from us. Set the house and shed afire!"

Over the bleating of the sheep being slaughtered came a growing crackling, as their cottage began to burn. The sad and eerie light of the pyre climbed the cloudy night sky and filtered dimly through the maze of trees to where Tom and his mother crouched in a thicket of bushes.

Nora Rhymer was crying softly, and Tom could not find it within him to silence her. At this moment, he hardly cared whether they were discovered or not.

Hours dragged by in drizzly misery. From the vicinity of their torched home came the sounds of boisterous, rowdy celebration. Tom could picture their sheep being devoured, bloody and charred, in the ghastly light cast by their burning cottage.

Eventually horsehoof thunder roused itself again. Loud at first, then dwindling to diminuendo, it signalled the departure of the rapacious invaders. Or so Tom hoped.

He whispered to his mother. "We must go back, Mother. Perhaps to rescue something from the wreckage. Then on to Uncle Ross's. It's all in the same direction. Come, Mother. Up to your feet."

Nora wordlessly complied. They began to make their way back, encountering obstacles they had barely noticed in their flight, such as face-high branches and tangled roots.

About a hundred yards from the clearing, Tom halted, a thought occurring to him.

"This might be a trick to capture us, Mother. I'll go with caution alone from here. If it's safe, I'll come back for you."

His mother said nothing, and Tom began to worry for her mind.

"Do you understand, Mother?" he asked gently.

As if dragging herself back from the darkside of the moon, she turned her night-hidden face to Tom.

"Yes. Yes, son. I'll wait."

"Good. I'll be only a minute."

Reluctantly, Tom released her hand and moved off.

At the clearing's edge, he saw that the devastation was worse than he had feared.

The ground was chewed up into a mucky mire. The buildings were a large and small heap of sizzling coals. Raw bones lay scattered, as if they had rained from a battle in the sky. The yard seemed truly deserted.

Tom turned to rejoin his mother.

Halfway back to her, a growing rumbling made itself apparent in the distance.

Hoofbeats.

More than before.

Tom rushed back to his mother's side. He found her under the sheltering pine he had picked as a landmark in the stygian woods. She was shivering, but seemed oblivious to her chill, making no move to chafe her arms or stamp her feet for warmth. Her face — what Tom could discern of it — appeared distant and abstracted, as if she were miles away and listening to voices Tom could not hear.

Restraining an urge to shake her, Tom approached and laid an arm around her shoulder.

"Mother," he said softly.

Tom's voice, combined with his touch, caused her shivering to cease. Heartened, he continued.

"There are more riders approaching."

Nora's shivers began again, more violent, as if she were in the grip of the ague.

"No, don't fear — I have a hunch our luck has turned. It sounds like a larger force, Mother. No doubt a group of aroused citizenry in pursuit of that madman. Who knows what other damage he's wrought in the countryside? I'm sure these newcomers will be our salvation. They'll spare a horse or two to carry us to Uncle Ross's. Who could begrudge us that?"

Not a word passed Nora's lips, but the spasms wracking her skinny frame lessened a bit, and Tom took heart.

"Just imagine, Mother. Riding like kings to Uncle's, and then sitting in front of a warm fire while we tell of our adventures. Let's be off."

They stepped out from under the closely woven umbrella of pine-needles, leaving its aromatic embrace. The rain was falling more steadily now, a cold and clammy insult heaped atop the other blows they had undergone. Tom adjusted his mother's cape — musky with sheep-scent — more closely around her neck, then tugged his own into a closer approximation of the unobtainable comfort that appeared a distant dream.

Moving slowly, they made their way back to the edge of their desecrated land.

Standing on the edge of their trampled property, listening to the thundering hoofbeats swell to a crescendo, Tom felt a curious sense of deja vu, as if he were stuck in a loop of time, forced to experience the same dreaded events again and again.

Once more, light preceded the riders.

This time, the torches cast a sharp white glare, unnatural in its intensity. It lit the path into the clearing in stark chiaroscuro, making the trees into spectral things composed of raw planes of light and dark. The shadows beyond the illumination seemed all the blacker in contrast, as if whatever strange material was burning gave off negative light, a kind of dark twin to the torches' component of normal radiance.

The uncanny glow seemed to race into the clearing of its own will, sucking the riders behind it like solid shadows.

Tom watched in wonder as men filled the far half of the yard. They were indeed a different party, and unlike the others, they did not encircle the clearing, but massed in a black blot that surged with suppressed energy like a bowl of ink shaken by a fussy child.

Their armor was uniformly black, save for white curlicued stripes outlining the joints. Their face-plates were all raised, revealing an assortment of dour visages, with nary a smile among them.

Their most curious feature was a certain compressed shape to their skulls, giving them the look of squashed pumpkins. Rather than crafting their headpieces to hide this common defect, the black warriors had fashioned their gear so as to accentuate the flatness of their skulls, as if it were a point of pride among them. And this deformity, instead of making the warriors appear ludicrous, gave them a bizarre, intimidating air, as if their motives might be as warped as their brainpans.

Those without flaming brands carried maces and crossbows. Each horse was a steed carved whole from an oily lump of coal.

When all the men had arrived, silence descended, save for the hiss of rain striking the failing embers of their home. Tom and his mother waited anxiously for some sign of the newcomers' intentions.

An individual trotted forward out of the clot. He raised high his party's banner: a black flag with a spoked wheel — a human figure bound to it — picked out in white. Following him came one whom Tom instinctively recognized as their leader.

The fellow was fully as big as the red marauder seen earlier. A flowing white beard that began high up on his cheeks concealed his features effectively.

Unlike his cohorts, his majestic head was unde-formed. He seemed too indomitable a presence to allow such mis-shapings of his body.

He gazed imperiously about the tragic scene before him, then called out loudly.

"Halloa, the survivors! If you be any, come forth and be succored!"

Tom's heart jumped in his chest like a caged bird beating its bars. He had been right! Their troubles were at an end!

Nora laid a hand on Tom's arm, as if to restrain him, but his eagerness leaped ahead of her.

"Here we are!" Tom shouted, stepping forward and waving his arms overhead. "Praise God you've arrived! We were almost ready to despair."

Their presence revealed, Tom's mother followed her son, knowing that to stay back would be useless.

The men and their leader regarded the bedraggled pair in complete and utter silence for a full minute. Tom's elation began to dissipate rapidly. He felt as if he and his mother were being weighed in a balance, some unknown quantity resting heavily in the other pan, devaluing their worth.

An owl's call broke the excruciating examination. As if the bird were a judge declaiming, "The jury may deliver the sentence," the bearded leader began to speak.

"The Bastard King has been here." There was no trace of interrogation in his voice. "His hand has lain heavily upon you."

Tom spoke up nervously. "Yes, yes indeed. You should have seen what that arrogant fellow did —"

Swords snicker-snacked out of sheaths and crossbows were cocked and lofted before Tom could finish. He stopped in mid-sentence, his jaw hanging open.

The leader regarded him sternly for several seconds, making sure Tom understood there were to be no more interruptions. Then he went on.

"When evil is abroad, it falls most often upon those with stained souls. The wholly pure, it avoids with the fearful abhorrence their saintliness inspires. We must each ask ourselves, when evil picks us as its victims, 'How have I failed to live up to the shining standards of the holy men and women — especially Him — who have come before us?'"

Tom stood benumbed. What did all this have to do with their plight? Couldn't these strangers see he and his mother just wanted a roof over their heads now, and perhaps a cup of hot broth? He wanted to shout all this out, but didn't dare.

"There is only one recourse when confronted with sin of such magnitude," the patriarchal figure observed, "both on the part of the King and those he has touched."

Here he paused, at last thundering:

"We must pray!"

With a gesture from the leader's gauntleted hand, his men dismounted, clamorously clanking. Two of them advanced on Tom and his mother, grabbed them by the shoulders, and forced them to kneel in the mud.

Meanwhile, the leader and the rest had all dropped down to an identical posture of reverence.

"Now," said the leader, "we will pray."

Tom's thoughts were shattered. He found himself unable to formulate a coherent idea. All that was real and meaningful was the cold slop soaking his lower legs, the rain beating on his bowed back and the hands at the base of his neck.

Half an hour crawled by. Suddenly, lightning and near-simultaneous thunder broke the sky in half, and a torrent poured out. Tom's hair was plastered to his skull, and he found it hard to breathe as water cascaded down his face. The kneeling men appeared not even to notice.

After a interval beyond measure, Tom heard his mother start to cough — deep, racking noises. The sound was too much for him to take, and he struggled to rise. Without apparent effort, the man behind him kept him pinned.

More time oozed by. Tom's rebellion subsided to apathy. He felt part of the primeval muck he knelt in. Nothing seemed to matter.

At last, he realized the pressure had departed his neck. Raising his head wearily, he saw the black-clad holy warriors preparing to mount. Tom clambered weakly to his feet. "Wait, wait," he called. "We've done what you asked. Take us to my uncle's home. It's not far."

The horse-borne men were already leaving. The leader was last, and he turned his majestic head back to say:

"The Lord helps those that help themselves."

Stupefied, Tom watched them depart. Rousing himself, he hastened to his mother. She knelt like a devotional display, her hands crabbed and mouth working silently.

Unable to make her rise and walk, Tom hoisted her on his back.

Without a rearward look, he began to trudge to his Uncle Ross's farm.

2

Travelling The Great Road

"How to get to fairy-land, by what road, I did
not know; nor could anyone inform me. . . further than that to reach fairy-land, it must be
voyaged to, and with faith."
— Herman Melville, "The Piazza"

Tick, said the chisel. *Tick. Tick. Tick.*

The stonemason kneeled under the brightly mocking
May sun, his baggy brown trousers stained with the
turned earth of the recently re-opened and re-filled
grave. With calloused hands, he delicately plied hammer
and chisel to form the name of Nora Rhymer beside that
of her husband, upon their mutual gravestone. Sharp
chips of stone spalled off under his tapping. His rough
features were knotted in concentration, laboring as he
did under the watchful eyes of his clients.

Tom stood with his uncle a few feet from the

graveside. The big man's arm was draped over Tom's shoulder in a gesture of consolation that went largely unnoticed by his nephew.

All Tom could think of at the moment was how the mason's awkward posture resembled his own humiliation that fateful night a month ago, when he and his mother had been forced into the mud by those insane crusaders.

Somehow he had survived all the inexplicable and undeserved traumas of that night, including the hazy, excruciating crawl of a trip carrying his limp and silent mother through rain and cold to Uncle Ross's steading. At the door of the dark house, at once familiar yet estranged by fatigue and confusion, Tom had laid his burden down, his muscles shaking. Somewhere he had found a last bit of strength left to knock. Within a minute or two, his Uncle had appeared, an axe cautiously upraised in one hand, a candle in the other. Sizing up the whole affair instantly, he had helped Tom and his mother inside, and immediately begun the task of nursing them back to health.

His simple and limited cure — getting them dry and warm, feeding them steaming turnip soup with barley — had sufficed to bring Tom back to health after a few days. The youth's constitution was equal to the task of battling the shock and cold he had undergone.

Nora Rhymer's case had been less hopeful from the start.

The morning after the attack and "rescue," she had awakened from her stupor just long enough to recognize her brother and son with a weak smile. Then, as if consigning all her share in life to these two men, she had lapsed back into fever and delirium. After a short interval, Tom and his Uncle had recognized symptoms of pneumonia in her labored breathing. Nothing they tried succeeded in averting the buildup of fluid in her lungs. Gradually, her breathing became a stertorous fourth presence in Ross's cottage, the sound of some evil imp sitting invisible on her chest. The painful noise of her gasping — a constant background accompaniment to their vigil — grated on the two men like the jeering of that same imp.

Nora had held out an impossibly long time — almost two weeks after the onset of the disease. Her inevitable death had came as both a release and sorrow.

The mason's loquacious tools uttered a final *tick*, and the inscription was finished. Transferring both hammer and chisel to his left hand, he rested his right upon the top of the granite headstone and levered himself up rather arthritically. Bad joints were the legacy of a thousand such carvings over a lifetime as the resident engraver of the small church that served those who lived too far from Ercildoune to attend services there.

Uncle Ross advanced upon the mason, to shake hands and press a more-than-generous sum into his horned and scratchy palm. Tugging the swatch of hair that crossed his brow, the man bid them farewell, turned and strode away, toward his tumbledown lodgings in one corner of the kirkyard.

Tom stood apart from the transaction, slightly guilty at leaving the whole affair to his uncle, yet also rather relieved at not having to deal with such necessary, if niggling details. His mind was still topsy-turvy from the entire concatenation of events, from seeing his double to burying his mother. He recalled how an inner voice had warned him, before he opened the door upon the apparition, that nothing would ever be the same thereafter.

Ruefully, he considered his nonspecific premonition, and found that it had understated the case rather than exaggerated. Like most delphic oracles, much relied on the interpretation of the hearer, and Tom had failed to put the fullest construction possible upon his intuition.

Looking up from his feet, Tom fully took in his surroundings for the first time since he had arrived to witness the engraving.

Beyond his parents' plot stretched a grassy acre dotted randomly with crazily leaning markers. The far edge of the cemetery was bounded by a small stream that purled along merrily among waving cattails and sedge. Shadowing the water were five or six willows up and down the marge. Their trailing foliage, like the disordered tresses of dryads, swept almost to the ground on one side, and into the brook on the other. The church — a sloping structure of fieldstones and slates, with moss growing ambitiously up from the foundation — hulked off to Tom's right like an understudy eager to play a part in the one-act tragedies enacted daily under its nose.

Without warning, the commonplace dimensions of the scene underwent a curious billowing and expansion. Successive translucent scales seemed to fall away from Tom's vision. Everything suddenly appeared to possess a supernal clarity, an intensification of self. It was as if Tom had made the transition to a higher plane of reality, identical in every respect to his old one, save for a lambent aura of vitality inhering in each mote. Each fragile blade of grass within Tom's vision, each willow-leaf and pebble, appeared at once to become diamond-bright and deep, comprising an infinite universe holding more wonders than a single mind could comprehend.

A robin landed at Tom's feet. Its crimson breast shone like fire. As if fully human, it tilted an intelligent, somewhat malicious eye up at Tom, who watched it as if it were the most miraculous thing in this new world.

The robin quickly dropped its head, poked its beak into the soil, and came up with a struggling black beetle. In one swift motion it tossed its head back and swallowed the bug. Seconds later, it retched and vomited the noxious beetle up unharmed in a puddle of bile. The bug trundled away.

As swiftly as the spell had come upon Tom, it vanished. Normal reality reasserted its quotidian nature. But a change remained. Tom was left feeling vastly different.

The uncertainty and pain and aching anomie that had filled him like cold porridge since the night of the terrors had dwindled to a small, tolerable knot of remorse and sorrow. His old life was not forgotten; such an oblivion was neither possible nor desired. His daily activities on the farm, his love for his parents, the love they had returned — all remained fresh and unbesmirched, a touchstone for the future. The advent of his doppleganger, or fetch, and the horrible treatment that had followed — these no longer inspired a cringing aversion and rage, but had been transformed into distant, ineluctable events that he could — well, certainly not cherish, but at least digest.

With a start, Tom found his fingers clenched tightly around the knobby crown of his walking stick, as on that distant evening. He regarded the short staff with wonder. It was one of two possessions that had emerged from his private holocaust. On the one and only visit he had made back to the ruins of his home, he had found the walking-stick lying partly hidden under last autumn's leaves a few feet into the woods, beside the wet, warped book of Master Alighieri's divine comedy. He had retrieved the objects unfeelingly, almost without thinking, and had brought them to his uncle's. This morning he had taken the length of hawthorn from its stand automatically, with equal lack of attention, as a lame man might grab his constant crutch.

Now, however, the stout stick — with its whorls where he had pared the branches from it, and copper-clad tip — seemed not a crutch, but an obvious token of his heretofore vague future.

Travel. Journeys. Distance. Discovery.

His uncle returned to his side, the mason paid. "Let's go, lad," he said. "We've a hearty lunch waiting at home."

They set out the kirkyard gate and down the narrow path among the trees that led to Uncle Ross's farm, among others.

As they walked, Tom regarded his uncle with his newfound perspective.

Ross Learmont was an affable bear of a man, easygoing and slow to anger, but an implacable force when riled. An inveterate bachelor, he maintained a trig and tidy farm whose specialty was turnips. The woody roots were everywhere on the farm, seeming to proliferate out of the very air. They hung from rafters and dwelled in the cellar. They bred promiscuously in the carefully cultivated soil and appeared floating in soups and stews. Even the door to the cottage was graced with twin representations of turnips, carved crudely into the frame by Ross.

Ross seemed to be doing his best now to act as if the unpleasantries of the past were finally buried with his sister. He talked of the summer festivals and fairs to come, of how he and Tom would raise a huge crop and reap the benefits at harvest. Tom let his uncle's rambling monologue parallel their meandering path among the oaks and birches, pines and yews, while he studied the man. Tom's debt to Ross was incalculable, and it pained Tom that what he was about to say would strike his uncle as daft and even, perhaps, ungrateful. But there was no recourse.

"Uncle," Tom interrupted, "I've come to a decision. I won't be staying with you any longer. In fact, I'm leaving this land entirely."

Ross came to an abrupt halt. They were in a small glade, and golden sunlight fell like spilled change from the pockets of angels upon the blades of emerald grass and the tiny white flowers that speckled the lawn. The aroma of moist earth filled their nostrils like poor man's perfume.

"What can you mean, lad? Have I been too harsh with you?"

Tom felt tears welling up in his eyes. "No, of course not, Uncle. If anything, you've bent over backwards to help. It's just that there's nothing here for me anymore."

Ross thumped his chest with a meaty hand, as if struck with remorse and inspiration. "It's your own place you want! How unlike old Ross, who values his own independence so, not to see it. All that good land's still yours, son. We'll gather the neighbors before you can blink, and have a house up for you in a day or three. And those fields — I always suspected they'd grow better turnips than mine. It's not too late to sow a crop —"

Tom grabbed his uncle's arm to calm him down. "Hold it, Uncle. That's not what I want either."

Ross was dumbstruck, having exhausted the possible conditions of life as he knew it. "What then, boy?"

"I'm going to travel, Uncle Ross."

Tom might as well have added that he was going to sprout wings to do it. His uncle eyed him with undisguised befuddlement, then ventured, "It's not revenge you've got in mind, is it, boy? For that's a hopeless case. You know what we found. Two kinds of tracks — different shoes on the horses, we agreed — appearing from nowhere in the middle of the Great Road, running straight to your house, then vanishing again. It was as if those devils materialized out of the empty sky, before heading direct to your place. How could you ever find them? No one here's ever heard of such disagreeable people within leagues of Ercildoune."

Tom had to look deep within before he could truthfully speak. "It's not revenge I seek. I like to think I'm above such actions, that mother wouldn't want her death balanced with others. No, it's — I'm after something else, Uncle. I just — In the kirkyard just now, I had a vision of another world, a place where everything's in harmony. I have to look for it."

Shaking his head, his uncle said, "An impossible task, boy. You'll break your damn fool heart at it."

Tom started to protest, but Ross cut in with a smile.

"Yet who the hell am I to naysay it? Let's hurry home and get one last hot meal inside you before you set out."

Clouds celebrated themselves overhead, fat flocculent whales swimming the cold upper air. The sun, an aureate brooch on the blue-white breast of the heavens, neared its noontime height. Zephyrs scented with vernal floral fragrances — lily-of-the- valley, hyacinth, lilac — teased the virginal leaves of the trees whose pleached limbs interlaced above the Great Road. The breezes, Tom thought, were like the sweet utterances of mysterious women, urging one to perform daring feats and prodigies.

As he walked happily along — bounced would perhaps have better described his movements — he swung his walking stick in wide arcs, striking the rutted dirt of the Great Road with a vigorous *thump* at the end of each swing, and then almost polevaulting himself along. The capacious leather scrip — hanging from a single strap over his left shoulder and across his back and chest, and banging on his right hip — seemed a negligible weight, although one might have regarded it as a house, since it carried everything Tom owned.

Tom could hardly believe what he was doing. His mind buzzed like a boxful of bees. To be on his own, striding down the Great Road, magisterial as a lord, carefree, albeit poor and unknown — this seemed to be what he had been dreaming of for over a decade. At last he was going to get the chance to find out what life was all about. The hidebound dichotomy enforced in the community of his birth and young adulthood was going to be put to the test. Feeling like a cunning artificer in

that most plastic of media, life itself, Tom knew —
although he couldn't say how — that he was going to
mold his way of being into a shining example of uncon-
ventional glory and exaltation.

Breaking into a gay whistle, Tom recalled his leave-
taking. Even that potentially painful situation had
proved not half so bad as he had feared.

His uncle had tried to press a moiety of his hoarded
gold and silver and copper into Tom's hands. Tom had
refused, explaining that he wished to survive by honest
work and wits, and not charity.

"All right, all right, then," Ross had fussily agreed.
"But surely you won't be such a mooncalf as will refuse
this!"

Ross jumped to his feet, crossed the room, reached
up to a high shelf, and brought down an object concealed at first by a cloud of dust. When the motes
cleared, Tom could see that his uncle held a rusty, naked
sword.

"Won in battle by my father," Ross said with immense pride. "And now yours."

He deposited the dulled blade with its corroded pommel ceremoniously in Tom's lap.

Up until the night of the disaster at the Farm, Tom
had never even seen a sword. No one he knew owned
or needed one. This keepsake of his uncle's had never
seen the light of day in his memory. Tom didn't like
swords, or dream of them, or cherish tales of them,
whether they were formed of magical substances or

simply plain iron. This one made him queasy, innocuous as it was.

"Uncle Ross," Tom temporized, "this is an honor."

Ross beamed, his grey eyes sparkling.

"But I can't accept it." Tom held the sword up for his uncle to take back. "_Primus_, I don't know the first thing about using one. _Secundus_, these advanced weapons are dangerous in and of themselves. Just owning one makes you more prone to use it. You remember your own talk about revenge, don't you?"

Unable to contravene Tom's arguments (and rather cowed by the Latin), Ross had wordlessly taken back the memento, and spoken no more of it, right up until he embraced Tom goodbye.

Which was why, as he strolled merrily along, Tom carried nothing more deadly than a little knife, useful only for dispatching an apple or loaf of bread from this mortal coil.

The Great Road stretched away before Tom like an invitation. He had never travelled this far along it before. Many times he had longed to accompany his father on a trading trip to Ercildoune, but had been ever denied. Harl Rhymer, in a few short sentences, had always dismissed the town as a sink of iniquity, not fit for his son.

This, of course, only made it all the more attractive, and Tom now looked forward to reaching it after another day's travel.

The Road suddenly left the shelter of the forest, and

entered upon an expanse of rolling terrain, covered with pastel-flecked gorses and heathers. The sun immediately asserted itself, raising a slick of sweat across Tom's brow. He wished that he had thought to stop for his midday meal in the shade of the woods, but it was too late now. Tom had no intention of taking a single backward step along this journey. He marched on, hoping that some lone tree would materialize, under which he could rest himself.

The tripartite Road — a rut, a central strip of moist grass, another rut — wended onward. After a time, up ahead, Tom spied what appeared to be a small copse, promising relief. He speeded up, eager to relax.

Coming closer, Tom realized that what he had thought to be a stand of small trees was in reality a cluster of huge rhododendron bushes. Each over ten feet tall, the bushes formed a sizable grove through which the Road arrowed. With their glossy leaves profusely growing upon their gnarly trunks — trunks thick around as Tom's upper arm — the bushes afforded the shade Tom had been anticipating.

Once among the bushes, Tom doffed his bag and sat dawn under the leaves with legs crossed. Rummaging in his bag, he came up with lunch: mashed turnip sandwiches, and a corked flask of dark beer.

Tom raised a sandwich to his lips. A heartrending moan sounded from deep within the bushes. Tom stopped. So did the moan. He peered keenly into the grove, but was unable to discern anything suspicious. He brought the sandwich again to his lips. No noise. Shrugging idly, he fell to eating.

When he was done, he burped contentedly and considered a nap. But the lure of distant wonders decided him against delay. He would allow himself just a minute's more rest.

His belly full, Tom noticed for the first time that the bushes were in bloom. Creamy white and pink flowers, big as his two cupped palms, festooned the branches. Scentless, they made up for this lack with their sheer visual extravagance.

Tom admired them for a moment, before noticing one bloom in particular. It was a unique carroty color, set back amid the others.

Fancying that the unique flower would look fine adorning his shirt, Tom stood limberly and shot forth his hand to grasp the bloom. With a tug, he sought to pluck it.

"Ouch!" cried the bush.

Tom jerked his hand back as if burned. This bush had definitely called out, as if in pain. Although never having encountered such a phenomenon before, Tom found it not unlikely that such a thing could be. Doubtless a species of dryad made her home in the bushes, and Tom had offended her. Lucky he was that these had not been apple trees, or he might have found himself bombarded with fruit thrown by a vengeful spirit.

Tom hastened to make amends. Bowing low, he said, "Forgive me, O gracious nymph of the mountain-laurels, for my trespass. Name a favor I might perform, in appeasement."

"Give me all your money," said the bush, in a tremulous falsetto.

Tom scratched his head. A most perplexing request, from a spirit of the nonhuman world. Yet how could one ever know what pleased such beings?

"Alas, I cannot comply, fair nymph, being coinless. Perhaps a snippet of my own hair, in recompense —"

The bush rustled, as if in consideration. Without warning, two lovely hands appeared, grabbed the branches and pulled them aside, like an actor parting a stage-curtain.

Tom fell back, awed at the possibility of meeting a beautiful nymph so early in his journey.

From the bushes stepped a man as skinny as the handle of a hoe. A mass of orangey-tawny curls topped his narrow head: the blossom Tom had sought as a corsage. The stranger's face was a composition of odd angular promontories, chief of which was a nose like the keel of a fast ship. Dressed in varying shades of scarlet, from silken neckerchief to elegant shoes, he was a study done by a painter with a limited palette, save for the extreme whiteness of his skin.

The stranger regarded Tom's startlement with an ironic look. His green eyes held more than a trace of manic wildness.

"Much as I admire your ebony thatch, my lad — so unlike my flamboyant crown — I would much

rather have one of those sandwiches you were munch-
ing."

Tom found his voice. "You — you were in the bushes
all along. There was no spirit."

The stranger laid a long slim finger alongside the
prow of his nose, which matched the finger in length. "A
perceptive youth. How rare in this degenerate age. Now,
if only your generosity matches your wit —"

Studying this monochrome peacock of a man, Tom
found no reason not to share his paltry victuals with
him. Accordingly, he dipped into his bag and came up
with his last sandwich.

The man snatched it as if starving, and devoured it
like a hyena. Alarmed that he might choke, Tom fished
out his flask, which the stranger promptly confiscated
and drained.

When finished, the man seemed more inclined to proceed with the proprieties of social intercourse, which he
obviously valued in a punctilious way. He made a sweep-
ing flourish, and announced himself.

"Natty Spurgeon at your service, sir. And you are?"

"Tom. Thomas Rhymer."

"Ah, a poet, by the sounds of it."

Flattered, Tom considered briefly accepting the des-
ignation — which had a strange charm in his ears — but
at last opted for the truth.

"No, not at all. Just a country boy, heading for Ercildoune and points beyond, seeking my fortune." On the
spur of the moment, and seeking to impress, Tom added,

"And bound by oath to discover a way to live in the world that defies convention!"

Natty clapped his hands together with an expression of sheer delight.

"Excellent! In all parts, you are a man after my own heart. I too am heading for Ercildoune, was once a simple lad from the boondocks just as yourself, and positively insist on flouting convention. I propose that we travel together, for mutual benefits both social and professional."

Warming to Natty's ingenuous demeanor, Tom heartily agreed. The two men shook hands on it, and set off down the Great Road.

The hours until sunset passed quickly, as the two companions crossed swales and hills, coombs and the bare backs of broad buried boulders, engaged in a witty banter the likes of which Tom had never before enjoyed. Natty's stock of anecdotes and repartee seemed deep as the cold waters of a far northern loch, and twice as stimulating. Tom found his own powers of conversation rising to the occasion, as his mind expanded under the liberating influence of his new-found friend. He felt almost drunk on words, inebriate of air, as he batted the shuttlecock of chatter back and forth. How true that old saw was: travel was broadening! Already, he felt a new and finer person, for having dared to leave the stifling security of the world he had always known.

Tom hardly saw the land they traversed as the afternoon waned. When he took full cognizance of his surroundings once more, it was the time of the dying of the sun, and he was positioned in a fine place to witness it.

The Great Road, after donning a skin of dun-colored cobbles, had borne them to the crest of a hill that rose up gradually from the tussock-dotted marshland spreading away in all directions. The hill was bald, save for a single majestic oak, bedecked with hanging moss, that grew at the top. Tom and Natty enjoyed a view of nearly three hundred and sixty degrees. Behind them, they could barely see a verdant smudge that represented the forest near Tom's home. Ahead, the Great Road — built, so it was said, with elaborate care by Roman legions long ago — was laid flat and straight as a rule across the treacherous bogs, in which the grey skeletons of dead trees stood like crucifixes awaiting thieves. Tom thought to detect a pinhead of smoke that just might represent Ercildoune.

In the west, the sun was vanishing. Reluctant to be forgotten, it stained the air with hues of carnelian and rose. The dye, touching the horizon line, seemed to be absorbed as if by blotting paper, oozing left and right as if to encircle their vantage, travelling almost the full circle to the sun's point of eastern arrival. The horizon looked like the rim of a bloody crown still worn by a decapitated tyrant.

After a moment of appreciation, Natty clapped a hand upon Tom's shoulder, "Well, my young *bonvivant*, we seem destined to rest beneath this poor shelter tonight. But at least we have the consolation of your bountiful wallet. Break out an encore of that fine repast, and let's fall to!"

"I'm afraid we finished my food at noon," Tom apologized.

"The beer also?"

Tom nodded.

A sourceless black shadow seemed to slide across Natty's face, rendering his affability into scorn and anger. Before Tom could be sure he had even such a thing, though, Natty was all smiles again, his jade eyes flashing.

"No matter. What is mere sustenance to philosophers such as we? No doubt you can provide us with a fire, at least, and then we shall enjoy a diversion of my making."

The fire sounded like a good idea to Tom, and together they gathered leaves and twigs from beneath the draped oak, snapped off enough dead branches to last the night, and soon had a blaze started, employing Tom's flint and steel.

When they were settled around it, Natty reached within his puffed sleeves and produced a pack of cards.

"I propose a game of chance I recently learned. Its rules are quite simple, and although I am a novice with cards, I believe I can impart them to you. First, we extract three cards from the deck."

With lightning speed, Natty dealt three gaudy pasteboards.

"Note that two are black — the Ace of Cups and the Deuce of Swords — and that one is red — the Knave of Candles. Now, if you will be so kind as to spread your bag flat, for a playing surface — Very good. I lay the three cards face down. Observe that the red card initially rests between the two black ones. This is when the game commences."

Tom had watched the procedure with interest, but remained puzzled. "Don't I get any cards?" he asked.

"Games where both players hold cards are rather too much for my limited wits, I fear. This is much less taxing. You simply watch as I maneuver the cards, then state which one you believe is the red Knave."

"That's it?"

Natty nodded. "Of course, if you desire to add spice to the play, we might wager same money an it."

Tom sighed with exasperation. "I told you already, I haven't any."

Negligently waving a manicured hand, Natty said, "Your promise of payment is as good as gold."

Tom considered. "Well, all right. Just once. I'll bet tuppence."

Natty opened his mouth as if to protest, then thought better of it. "Fine, tuppence," he grumbled. Then his hands flew like birds. The cards flickered in place, seeming not even to move. "Done," Natty announced.

Bewildered, Tom hazarded an almost random guess. "The Knave is the card on my left."

Natty flipped the card, revealing the Ace of Cups.

"Sorry, my friend. You should have watched more closely. Let's try again. This game requires some practice."

Natty's hands again wove like the winds. Tom made his choice: the card he picked, however, showed itself to be the Deuce. Tom's confusion began to shift to anger.

Again, the flashing hands, the revelation: another black card, two more pence lost. Tom's anger suddenly threatened to overflow.

"I don't like this game," he said. "Already I owe you six pence I don't have. Getting into debt is not what I set out to do."

Recognizing Tom's implacability, Natty sought to appease him. "My friend, consider the debt discharged. My intention was only to amuse you. Surely you will grant that."

Tom softened. "I suppose." An idea struck him. "Listen, I have a game in my bag that's more suited to friendly play."

Digging within the former cardtable, Tom came up with a little hinged chest fastened with a clasp. He opened the box, revealing two sets of flat round pieces — red and black — and a painted surface of sixty-four red and black squares.

"Dambrod," Tom said, "although I've heard the English call it draughts."

Natty made a faint sneer. "Very well. I don't suppose —"

"No bets."

Reluctantly, Natty agreed to play. His first game was *pro forma*, his second desultory, his third barely sentient, and Tom grew bored. They agreed to call it a night and go to sleep.

The temperature being mild, and Tom, for some unanalyzable reason, not wishing to share his hidden blanket with Natty, they both curled up uncovered, beside the dying fire.

As he was falling asleep, Tom had a heart-wrenching start, as his drifting mind flashed a picture of Natty stabbing him in the night and making off with his wallet. But he dismissed the figment as unjust suspicion, and soon fell asleep.

In the morning, Tom awoke first. Natty was still dozing, and Tom's meager possessions were intact. He congratulated himself on relying on a policy of faith in his fellow man.

Natty soon awoke, somewhat querulous, and they departed their camp.

A bit before noon, they came upon a clean cool stream — the land was becoming less swamp and more pasture — and sated their thirst. Otherwise their stomachs remained empty, and they hastened on toward Ercildoune.

At dusk, they reached the periphery of the town. Both men were tired and sullen, hungry and footsore. Tom thought of all the times he had rehearsed this scene in his mind, arriving proudly, dawn breaking, at the first real stop in his journey, ready to conquer it like Caesar.

Now that the moment was actually at hand, all he desired was a crust of bread and a place to sleep. Due to the gathering gloom, all he could see of the village was the muddy thoroughfare underfoot and the blank-faced walls of the houses to either hand.

Tom spoke up first, "I'm going to look for a stable, where perhaps the owner will let me bed with the horses."

Natty sniffed. "Such a berth was not what I had in mind. But although quite able, I am reluctant to pay the exorbitant charges the innkeepers of this town demand. I will accompany you, and mayhaps we can convince your hypothetical hostler to give us some supper as well."

Trudging on in silence, Tom leaning heavily on his cane, they took aleatory branches in the maze of streets, and soon found themselves in a poorer section of Ercildoune. Here the houses were ramshackle and lacking whitewash. Trash was heaped against walls and a pervasive odor of animal and human urine underlay a myriad less identifiable odors. Public torches were almost non-existent.

Tom despaired of ever finding someone who would put them up for the night. He felt like walking straight out of the town, without ever having really seen it, and camping again on the Great Road, where at least the air was fresh.

Rounding a corner, his heart low, Tom saw the unexpected glare of torches bracketed on either side of the door of a long, low building. Jumbled noises, muted by distance and walls, floated through the night like vapors above a fetid pool. A sign hung from a leaning post-and-arm outside the door. As they approached, Tom could make out its lettering:

BURDOCK'S BOWER OF DESIRES
AND
FISH SHOP

A sharp clap sounded from beside Tom, and he jumped. But it was only Natty, applying palm to forehead.

"Of course!" Natty exclaimed. "My old friend, Burdock! How could the presence of his illustrious tavern have slipped my mind? I stand humbled, a man losing his grasp."

"You know the owner of this place?" Tom asked.

"Of old," Natty replied. "We were comrades before you were born. Burdock owes me many a favor — not the least of which was saving his life once. When we make ourselves known to him, he will fete us like royalty, at no cost."

Tom was moved nearly to tears. Here was his reward for befriending a stranger: to receive succor when most needed and least expected. Cast your bread upon the waters, indeed!

Natty gripped Tom by the elbow, saying, "Let's not dally with solace in sight, my lad."

They hurried toward the hostel, Tom imagining their boisterous reception.

Natty opened the door on its creaking iron-strap hinges and motioned Tom to precede him. Tom stepped across the portal.

The fishy, smoky interior was lit dimly by scattered cressets. Round scarred tables, their tops nearly obscured with tankards, were scattered like pieces in a game of Dambrod without rules. At the tables hunched or roistered various villainous men, a few of them accompanied by rather coarse women.

Tom took another step in, and Natty followed, shutting the door. Patrons — those not in a stupor — looked up briefly, neither hostile nor friendly, then turned again to their own concerns.

A mop of bristly hair suddenly appeared at the level of Tom's waist. He looked down.

A hunchbacked dwarf, clutching four tankards in his knuckly fists and wearing a spatted apron, said, "Your pleasure, mates?"

Natty fell upon the little man with the devotion usually reserved for holy maddonas, causing beer to slop from the dwarf's cargo of cups. "Burdock, you rascal! Not changed a bit since we last met! It's so wonderful to lay these weary eyes on your charming face once more."

The dwarf regarded Natty as if he had opened his mouth and spouted a flock of bats. "Ye're daft, or drunk already, old sot. The name's Noll. If ye want me to fetch Burdock —"

Natty straightened with great aplomb. "My mistake,

fellow. It won't be necessary to beseech your master. Just show us to the best table in the house."

Harumphing, Noll said, "I've these drinks to deliver. Find an empty table yourself, and pretend it's the best."

Noll left.

"I've a good mind to report his sass," Natty asserted. "However, we'll chalk it up to overwork. Come, Tom, let's sit."

Tom and Natty, seeing no empty seats, were at a loss, until Natty dispossessed a snoring man from his chair onto the sawdust-strewn floor, and claimed the vacant table. Eventually Noll came and took their orders for pigs-feet, broad beans and ale. When their meal arrived, they fell to like condemned men.

At last satisfied, they sat up and idled comfortably over the remainder of their beer like men, instead of wolves.

A burly man across the room yelled out above the noise, "Say, Burdock, my beer's been watered down!"

At the door that must have led to the kitchen, a man paused in mid-step. He was six feet tall, had a belly like a wheel-barrow full of suet and a port-wine birthmark across half his face.

"Don't piss in h'it no more, then!" Burdock yelled. The crowd roared, and the burly complainer fell silent, chagrined.

Tom opened his mouth in amazement, about to inquire of Natty how he had possibly mistaken Noll for the enormous innkeeper. But his friend was no longer there. Tom spied him across the room, sauntering toward another door, neither the kitchen one nor that leading out.

Hastily grabbing bag and stick, Tom jogged after him.

At the door, he caught Natty by the shoulder.

"Where are you going?" Tom said.

"I heard someone mention there was entertainment back here," Natty said without obvious guile, "and I thought I would attend. Knowing your own refined tastes, however, I hesitated to invite you."

Without definite proof of wrongdoing, Tom elected to maintain his faith in Natty for a while longer. Emboldened with drink, he said, "I'm game for anything you are. Let's see what they've got."

Natty shrugged. "As you wish."

Pushing aside a ripped and soiled arras that served as door, they moved to the next room.

Men clustered yelling around some hidden spectacle. Shouldering their way to the inner edge of the circle, Tom and Natty saw what so excited the spectators.

A knee-high ring of planks had been erected at the center of the room. Within the circle, two cocks fought. One was red as a maple leaf, the other black as a torturer's heart. Both wore nasty spurs, with which they raked at each other, drawing blood. Clinking a pouch full of coins, the gamemaster made the rounds, taking wagers on the outcome.

Natty called out, "Five shillings on the red!"

"Let's see the color of your silver, Carrot-top," the gamemaster replied.

"I'm good for such a piddling sum, my man. And please cease all references to the shade of my thatch."

The gamemaster — a lumpy fellow with pocked skin — thrust his face almost against Natty's. "What do you take me for? Forget it! Cash up front is house rules. And if I want to claim your mother mated with a carrot, I will."

Swifter than thought, Natty's fist came up and connected with the offensive face. The gamemaster shot backwards, was caught behind his knees by the ring, and toppled over atop the battling birds. The cocks shot up into the air, spattering the crowd with chicken blood.

Mass confusion ensued. In the melee — shouts, a dozen separate fistfights, demands for money back — Tom became separated from Natty. When he worked his way by crawling under the worst of the battle back to the commonroom, that filial defender of maternal honor, Natty Spurgeon, was nowhere to be seen.

Tom returned to his table. The drunkard still slept soundly beneath on his bed of sawdust. Tom wiped anxious sweat from his brow and sat.

In a minute or so, a clump of angry gamblers had formed around his table.

"Where is he?" one demanded. "That fox what ruined our game?"

"I don't know," Tom said. "I had nothing to do with it. That should be plain to anyone."

The men murmured among themselves, and came to a reluctant agreement. "Well, you may be blameless, but we still want your friend. If you see him, we needs to know. And we'll be watching. So don't try hooking up again with him on the sly."

Scuffling off, the men cast angry glances over their shoulders, like a bunch of paranoid owls.

Tom sat and waited. Natty failed to reappear. The night wore on. Tom drank too much.

A fat shadow fell upon him. Tom raised his eyes. It was Burdock.

"Closing time," the man growled. "Your bill h'is four guineas, what with breakage and h'all."

"Ah, of course," Tom said. "My friend — and yours — Natty Spurgeon, will be here in just a second to settle with you."

"Never 'eard of 'im."

Tom mouthed the innkeeper's words silently. They were the very ones he had been dreading.

"I'm afraid — That is —" Tom gulped. "No money."

Burdock raised one hammy fist. Three bruisers appeared from the very floorboards.

"Show 'im the street, boys."

Two men picked Tom up, chair and all. He sat stiff as one of Burdock's salted cods. They brought him to the door and heaved. Tom landed out in the putrid muck. The specialist enforcer who had done nothing heretofore came to where Tom lay and gave him a severe drubbing with Tom's own walking stick.

Bruised, dejected, insensible to his condition, Tom buried his face in the slimy street and wished the mud were deep enough to drown him.

3

Woman On Greensward

"Where willing Nature does to all dispense
A wild and fragrant innocence;
And fauns and fairies do the meadows till
More by their presence than their skill."

— Andrew Marvell,
"The Mower Against Gardens"

"Oof!"

Suddenly Tom took an interest in his surroundings again. A boot had caught him in the lower ribs, causing him to raise his grubby face from the street and grunt. The kick was not hard, nor did it seem deliberate. Apparently, someone crossing the road had stumbled upon him in the tenebrous early-morning hours.

An exclamation followed Tom's pained outburst.

"Hey, what's this, then? Look here, fellows, it's some

bugger sleeping it off where a horse could dash his brains out — if he has any."

Laughter greeted this depiction of Tom as an addled tosspot. It roused him to sit up and defend himself.

"I'm not drunk or brainless, you oafs. I'm the victim of yonder innkeeper, who failed to understand that my intentions were honest. I was as much a dupe as he."

Brusque hands in his armpits soon aided Tom to stand. He dabbed ineffectually at his fouled clothing. Surprisingly, his condition seemed to have evoked honest sympathy. Out of the murk was thrust his shoulder-bag and stick. Tom received them gratefully, uttering thanks. He strained his eyes to discern his rescuers. The torches behind him, on the exterior wall of Burdock's Bower, were guttering low, but afforded enough light to recognize the faces of many of the men who had been patronizing the Bower earlier. Apparently closing time had found them still full of piss and vinegar, and they were now departing en masse for other haunts.

Recognition was mutual. The man who had complained of watered beer said, "It's that dumb cove what was tricked by Carrot-top, like the rest of us who lost all our bets. Ye're in luck, lad. We're out to hunt that varlet down and take some satisfaction out of his hide. Come along and get your share."

Shouts and catcalls affirmed everyone's zeal for the project. Tom, however, could summon no zest for humbling Natty, who — for however brief a time — he had counted as his friend.

"No, no," Tom said. "I'm too sore for more activity tonight."

A wizened oldster pushed forward and leered at Tom. "There's wimmin in it too, boy. Maybe that'll stir your blood."

Cheerful encouragements followed the codger's announcement. "Rescue our whores!" "Break up the false convent!" "Greedy prig, that Shiverick!" "Lynch the clenchpoop!"

Seeing Tom's confusion, the beer-critic sought to explain. "There's a travelling preacher come to town in the last week who's been trying to make all our trollops go straight, offering 'em shelter and prayers. There's hardly a roundheels to be bought of late — as ye may've noticed from the lack of lasses working the Bower tonight. When we find his den, we're going to show Master Preacher the error of *his* ways."

Roars of acclaim greeted this fine speech, and, without further delay, the crowd streamed away, eager as pigs at a trough. Tom was left alone.

Recalling the warning about being run down by a horse, Tom retreated to the far side of the street, opposite Burdock's Bower, and sat down, his back against a wall, his head hanging between his upraised knees. He tried to collect his senses and decide what to do next.

The thing that rankled most, he decided, was how his faith had been betrayed. He had set out from home, full of high hopes, with a determination to treat all his fellow men fairly, relying on respect and a deep, insightful understanding of their individuality. There was to be no easy categorizing into roles such as saint or sinner. By so doing, he had imagined, he would bypass conventional strictures and pitfalls, establishing that bright middle way beyond good and evil that he longed for.

But the world refused to cooperate with his ambitions. He had been betrayed.

Tom resolved then and there to be more cautious, still without falling into cynicism. What he sought — the glory of a world in harmony — *must* be obtainable. Feeling he had made some small progress, he raised his eyes with the thought of getting up and moving on, despite his enervating fatigue.

An ebony specter without a face stood beside him. When it saw Tom's appalled gaze, it moaned, "Far from home, and all alone . . ."

Tom was petrified. His muscles felt like the gelatin left after boiling beef bones. He wanted to sink into the earth and never emerge. Then the spectre removed its head.

Tom closed his eyes and prayed.

When he opened them, he saw only a man.

The fellow wore a black wool cape that trailed all the way to the ground. In one hand that emerged from a slit in the garment, he held an enormous, broad-brimmed black hat. This hat, worn upon his downward-tilted head, must have obscured his features as he regarded Tom.

Strength flowed back into Tom's frame, and he stood. An earthly opponent he could deal with.

"Beware, sir," Tom warned. "I won't be taken advantage of again."

The man glanced heavenwards beseechingly. "O Lord," he exhorted the night sky in a bass drone, "what evil times these are, when men tend to see a robber instead of a Samaritan."

Tom still remained defensive. "A visitor can't be too careful in this town. How do I know your motives are honest?"

"'By their fruits ye shall know them,'" the morose stranger countered. "Trust yourself to my hands, and I will prove myself your friend, as I am to all the downtrodden."

Tom kept silent.

"I ken by your appearance that you must have been sorely abused," the stranger said earnestly. "But you cannot crawl into a shell. I offer only a safe, dry place for you to rest yourself for the night. Let me make amends for the transgressions of my fellow townsmen."

Considering the offer, Tom suddenly experienced the chill and dampness of the May night. His clothes were soaked, and he feared catching a cold or, worse, taking fever. Hadn't he just made up his mind to be wary without being mean-spirited? With only a moment's hesitation, he decided to accept the man's proffered shelter.

"I'll come with you, if there are no strings attached," Tom said.

"Praise the Lord," the man fervently declaimed. "Follow me, my son."

Tom and the erstwhile specter moved away from the building Tom had huddled against, down the street past Burdock's. When they came abreast of the feeble torches, Tom took advantage of the glow to observe his new-found savior.

The man's face was long as a horse's. His jaw resembled the square handle of a shovel. Webs of frown-lines anchored each corner of his lips. Nestled amid the hairs of his left eyebrow was a big brown mole like a raspberry drupelet. His hair was black as Tom's own.

Donning his hat and plunging his visage into blackness, the man began to talk.

"My name is Nathan Shiverick," he said. (Tom wondered for a second where he had heard that last name before, but the man's flood of speech soon bore Tom's thoughts onward.) "I was born far from here, but have been a wanderer since my youth. The community of my birth was a pious one, and I absorbed the virtues of its teachings along with my mother's milk. When I reached a certain age, I realized that the world beyond my town was not as enlightened as me and my family and fellow townsmen. In fact, I learned that it was a place of confusion and sin, where men stumbled in the dark for want of divine guidance.

"Reasoning that my happy and moral village had less need of me than the world did, I soon embarked on a peripatetic ministry which I have continued to this day.

Many are the miles I have roamed, seeking always to shed a little light on the heathen conditions I have found. When my ministrations are accepted, and I am sure that they will be continued in my absence, I move on, eager to spread my God-given inspiration across the land. I am mindful of the Lord's injunction about keeping one's light under a bushel."

Tom began to feel he had made a wise choice in accompanying Nathan. Although a trifle dour, the black-cloaked man seemed to be honestly concerned with his welfare.

"What sort of good works do you do?" Tom asked, more out of politeness than interest.

Nathan seemed flattered — if one could judge by a slight twitching of his stern, compressed lips. "There is my preaching, of course — hours and hours of it. That is paramount, to convert the hearts of the sinners. But I believe in tangible works also. We must always strive to alleviate the sad physical conditions most men suffer under. Mine is a theology of total liberation, both spiritual and bodily. Witness my current project in this town."

"What's that?" Tom asked.

"You shall see," Nathan replied mysteriously.

Tom held his questions as they trudged through the lonely, deserted streets.

At last they arrived at a nondescript two-story building with a half-timbered, stuccoed front, its windows all boarded up. Nathan stopped.

"I would like to place a proud sign here," Nathan said, "as a beacon indicating refuge. 'Shiverick's Sanctum for Wayward Ladies.' But alas, the citizens of this ignorant town are too benighted to understand my work, and I must labor on in obscurity."

Nathan withdrew a rattling ring of keys from beneath his mantle. Fitting one to a padlock, he soon had the door open. Tom was ushered inside, and the door was relocked from within.

The first thing Tom noticed was an overpowering odor of perfume. The interior of the house held a mixture of all the cheap scents invented since Cleopatra. Combined with his lack of sleep, the heady atmosphere made Tom dizzy. He was hardly prepared for the loud shrieks that sounded immediately behind him, and threatened to lift the top of his skull.

"Oooo, Nate, lovey, ye're back!"

A horde of billowy silk-clad fleshy women descended upon Tom and Nathan. Tom was lifted off his feet, spun around and petted by dozens of hands before he could take any action to rescue himself.

Nathan's powerful voice boomed out. "Here, here, ladies! Cease and desist! What kind of behavior is this, from those who call themselves reformed? Set this man down. He's no plaything for your wicked ways, but a soul in distress, as you all were before I intervened."

"Don't be so *croo-ul*, Nate," female voices chimed. "We didn't mean nothing by it."

Tom was set down on his unsteady feet. Looking around, he saw that he had been manhandled by as varied an assortment of trulls, mattress-backs, jades, tarts, placket-openers and ladies of generally bad reputation as one could ever hope to meet, all in various stages of undress. In short, his gentle assailants comprised all the missing whores of Ercildoune, immured here, seemingly with their consent, by the Reverend Nathan Shiverick.

Before Tom could pay his respects to the wayward ladies, Nathan, candle in hand, had shuffled him up a flight of stairs to the second floor, and down a corridor. At the end of the passage — Tom believed they were at the rear of the house, but couldn't be sure — Nathan used his keys to unlock a door. Inside, in the light cast by a taper Nathan quickly lit, Tom encountered a pleasant room: bed, bowl and pitcher of water, wooden chest for clothes. A boarded window stared blankly back at him.

"This is the shelter I promised you," Nathan said. "Does it agree with you?"

The bed looked like heaven. Tom could only nod. Nathan said, "Very well. Give me your muddy clothing, and I'll have the girls clean it. They must learn to contribute to the ministry."

Tom stripped to the skin, eager to get beneath the bed's coverlets.

"Sleep well," Nathan said, clutching the bundle of besmeared linen and cotton. He left, shutting the door. Then Tom heard an alarming sound.

Nathan was fastening the lock.

Tom rushed to the door. "Hey," he shouted, pounding, "don't lock me in!"

From beyond the door came Nathan's mournful drone. "You must understand, boy. I can't have any hanky-panky going on under my roof. It's for the good of your own soul."

Tom forced himself to be calm. What else could he do? He laid himself down to sleep. Instantly slumber overhauled him.

Noise pried his heavy lids reluctantly open. Obviously, some time had elapsed. Minutes, seconds, hours? Who could say? The forgotten taper still burned, however, and no light of dawn filtered through the cracks in the boarded window.

Tom crawled wearily from bed. He felt vulnerable while naked. Perhaps the chest —

Inside the box, he found a pair of pants and a pullover smock. The pants ended at his knees; the arms of the smock extended beyond his fingertips. The pants he could do nothing about; the arms he rolled up.

Tom put his ear to the door. The noise was growing in volume. Tom thought to hear random disturbing words, such as "kill" and "burn." Then a battering began. Something thudded rhythmically against the front door.

The screams of the women started then. They were quickly followed by hurried footsteps and alarums.

Tom banged on the door. "Shiverick! Let me out!"

No response. Tom spun frantically about.

The window. Dragging the chest against the outside wall, he swore, using words Uncle Ross had inadvertently taught him. Standing on the chest, he was level with the frame. He began to kick at the planks.

They yielded reluctantly. Tom kicked harder. Flechettes of wood shot out into the night. Soon, two or three boards followed whole. Tom looked out. An alley, open on either end, the ground twelve feet below.

Simultaneous with Tom's victory, the party below gained entrance. Tom retracted his head and heard their shouts more clearly:

"Find Shiverick!" "Free the doxies!" "Burn the place!"

Tom grabbed his shoes, bag and stick, cast one despairing look at the soft bed, then mounted the chest and lowered himself out the window. Jagged boards drove splinters into his palms. He dropped.

Landing with bone-jarring force, he scrambled quickly to his bare feet. Screams issued from the house. Tom felt like a witness to the rape of the Sabine women. Without warning, flames sprouted behind the boards of the first-floor windows.

Tom turned and limped away into the night as fast as he could.

Tom dreamed he was the prophet Elijah. He was lost in the wilderness, starving, nearly delirious, and he called

unto the Lord for help. Instantly ravens arrived croaking
from nowhere, carrying berries in their beaks wherewith
to feed him. They alighted on his shoulders and out-
stretched arms, their talons prickling his skin through
his hairshirt like dozens of knifepoints. He began to
stagger under their weight, as more and more arrived.
"Okay, thank you, Lord, that's enough," he called out in
his dream. But it availed naught. Still the ravens flapped
in and settled upon him. Even his bald, holy pate became
a perch for the birds. At last he could keep his balance no
longer and fell over. Lying on his back, he felt the birds
walking up and down him as if he were a carpet.

Tom awoke. He looked up from his supine position
into a canopy of leaves. He realized something was
standing on his chest. Chin butting his collarbone, he
strove to see what it was.

It was a crow big as a lapdog. It stood atop Tom with
a speculative air. In its beak was a ladybug, red as a drop
of blood.

The crow seemed to realize that Tom was awake. It
hopped forward on his chest, and tried to feed him the
ladybug, poking its hard beak between Tom's lips.

Tom was disgusted. "Ack! Shoo! Get out!" Tom
waved his arms and the crow desisted from its corvine
charity. It flew away, cawing hilariously.

Sitting up, Tom took in his surroundings with the air
of a man recovering from a week-long drunk. The bewil-
dering events in Ercildoune had affected him as strongly
as a gill of hard spirits.

The corrugated boles of trees were all around him, interspersed with thickets and shrubs, which served to damp his vision after a few yards in hazy green foliage. Beside him on his decay-redolent bed of leafmold rested his stick and bag. Birds sang and trilled — a chorus of idiots, he thought sourly. Early morning light — soft and gauzy as a bride's veil — lay over the whole scene.

Tom stood with creaking muscles. His clothes were dew-moist, his hair full of forest-duff. Dried cracked mud tightened the skin of his face: a treatment queens no doubt paid good money for, but one he could have done without.

He tried to remember how he had come here. At first memory played the mute. Then it spilled all, in vivid detail.

Limping away from the burning building that had housed Shiverick's mission, stopping only long enough to don his shoes, Tom gradually built up speed, convinced that the whole town would soon be on his tracks. Having, by then, gone almost twenty-fours hours without sleep (save for the few blessed minutes in the Sanctum for Wayward Ladies), he found his thoughts becoming increasingly incoherent. All he could concentrate on was fleeing this night-shrouded town that had so vastly disappointed him.

Somehow he had came upon the Great Road where it exited Ercildoune, on the far side of the village from his entry-point. He had really kicked up his heels then, making the most of the straightaway, but at the same time feeling exposed to the view of any pursuers. After an hour or so, his strength began to wane. At the same time, he heard — or imagined — the sound of hooves behind him.

Desperate, he plunged off the Road and into the surrounding woods. He thrashed his way through the bosky darkness, getting raked across his bare calves by briars and slashed across his face by branches. An image of the flight he and his mother had been forced to take on another star-crossed night came back to him. Was this to be his destiny then, to race pell-mell through one *selva oscura* after another, when all he wanted was to find the key that would allow him to recover the clarity of his kirkyard epiphany?

No answer revealed itself, and presently even the question disappeared in a fog of exhaustion. Tom collapsed to the floor of the woods and fell almost instantly asleep.

Scratching his itchy, dirty skin now, Tom considered his position and his plans — if any — for the future.

Were things really as glum as they appeared? Definitely not! He still had his bag full of tokens from home — chief of which was the volume of profanely holy poetry — and his trusty walking stick. True, the wonderfully comfortable garments sewn lovingly by his departed mother's own hands were no more than ashes in the smoldering ruins of Shiverick's Sanctum, and he no doubt looked like a very poltroon in his present outfit. But he still had his goal, his dreams, the truly important things. Just as he had internalized the bad things that had befallen him earlier, at home, and emerged a better person for it, so would he seek the core of wisdom at the center of the rotten apple of what had happened last night.

Feeling a renewed vigor and determination, Tom next began to rank his actions in order of immediacy. First, perhaps a drink and a bath at a delightful pond or brook. Next, return to the Great Road and —

The Great Road. In which direction did it lie?

Frantically, Tom looked for signs of his passage in the surrounding foliage. Nothing. Out of all the twigs he had snapped, not one showed now. The springy floor held no footprints. It was as if the forest were a sea which had closed behind him, trackless and vast.

His galvanized gaze falling on an oak with accessible lower branches, Tom quickly scrambled up its height, seeking literally to rise above his predicament. Poking his head at last above the topmost leaves, Tom searched for the Great Road. There was no trace of it. It might just as well have vanished overnight, for all it showed now. The sun plainly revealed which way was east, but what good did that do him, when he had no idea in which direction he had blundered?

Disheartened, Tom descended.

On the ground, he recovered his bag and stick and set out randomly, hoping to come by sound or smell upon a stream which he could follow to civilization.

Minutes piled themselves one atop another, like drowning ants, until they became hours. Hours — more ponderous, like mating elephants — eventually gave birth to that time known as noon. The sun stood high, seeming to smile upon Tom's discomfort.

Tom had come upon no source of water. His throat and mouth were parched, his grubby hide even more repellent than it had been this morning. He felt like a horse that had been whipped along for miles, then left uncurried and unfed.

Determining to refresh his soul, if not his body, Tom stopped and sat in the shade of an elm. Lifting the flap of his pouch, he reached within and came up with Master Alighieri's wonderful text, that long saga of heaven and hell that had so entranced him for years.

Dipping into the book at a chance-revealed page, he began to read. But the familiar words blurred beneath his suddenly misty vision, and lost all their meaning. Where was his Virgil, his Beatrice? Why was he wandering alone and friendless? Even the hypocritical camaraderie of Natty Spurgeon or the overweening solicitude of Nathan Shiverick would be welcome at this point.

Tom bowed his head and began to weep.

Strings, plucked by unseen hands, plucked at his ears. Tom staunched his tears and lifted his streaky face. Was he truly hearing a harp, or had hunger caused him to hallucinate?

The plangent notes washed over him, like celestial balm. Flowing together into an ethereal strain, the notes seemed music evoked from silver strings. He was dying — that had to be it. Soon the fiery chariot would descend and whisk him away. Well, at least it wasn't the denizens of the other place coming for him.

The next second he wasn't so sure.

The skirly notes of a pan-pipe joined those of the empyreal harp. Lightly mocking, defiant, satyric, the gay braggadocio of the pipe twined in and out of the stately harp melody. It sounded as if two musicians, one supernal, one infernal, were waging a musical battle for his soul.

Tom listened to the competitive duet for a timeless time. Without warning, a score of other instruments joined in. Bassoons, violas, bagpipes, drums, hautboys, oboes, lutes, flutes, tabors, zithers, dulcimers, and flageolets were among those Tom thought he could recognize. The resulting symphony managed to unite the two previous themes. No longer could Tom's ear detect separate leitmotifs of innocence and evil. Somehow the disparate musical forces had been fused into a syncretic music unlike anything Tom had ever heard. It spoke to him of all he was questing for. Had his vision in the cemetery been accompanied by song, this would have been it.

Stuffing his book unconsciously back into his bag, Tom stood and moved toward the invisible orchestra.

His feet carried him without conscious direction through the forest. The music swelled, overpowering his ears, making him giddy with sonic liquor. Ahead, interwoven twiglets from adjacent bushes formed a screen in his path. The symphony seemed to derive from beyond this final lattice.

Tom reached the leafy screen. He laid his hands upon it, ready to part the branches and gaze upon this miracle. Suddenly, he paused.

He had unwillingly remembered his encounter with Natty in the rhododendron grove. Then, his heart had leapt, expecting the appearance of a nymph. Instead he had got Natty. Would he be similarly disappointed now?

The music cajoled him. "Come," it seemed to beckon. "Come hither all ye who thirst for no mortal waters."

Tom parted the bushes.

A vision seared his gaze, etching itself instantly and forever in its entirety on his retinas.

He looked into a languid lea, a secluded dell or patch of clear ground, covered with grass so green it seemed that each distinct blade was a small emerald flame. Impossibly, the blades far across the clearing burned as plain and sharp-edged as those immediately before him.

The greensward rolled away from Tom in a small hillock that occupied the center of the bower. The hillock was surrounded on three sides by flowers, like a natural amphitheater open to Tom. Cinnamon-speckled ferns formed a border at its base.

No natural planting, however, the garden held dozens of flowers, all in bloom, which never blossomed simultaneously in the world Tom knew.

There were irises, tawny, purple and white. Bluebells nodded like sleepy children. Yellow delphiniums soared like leonine sentries. Hollyhocks were whimsical creations in colored tissue. Balloon-flowers, as yet unopened, looked like azure party-favors. Coral-bells waved back and forth, as if to evoke chimes from their puckered rosy mouths. Daisies were the plain-janes at this formal floral ball. Among their sturdier sisters twined morning-glories and pale moon-flowers. Parrot-tulips with fluttery edges were sipped by darting hummingbirds. Lilies trumpeted: orange, cream and pink. Banks of honeysuckle discharged invisible clouds of fragrance which stood out from the generalized perfume that filled the glade.

At the crest of the gentle ferny brae were two rose bushes: one bore cabbage-sized flowers red as spilled entrails; the other, black blossoms like clots of night. Their thick, thorny canes arched up and over, till they met and sought to strangle each other.

Beneath this living arch lay a woman.

She wore a flowing green robe of silk, embroidered with silver vines. Dainty felted olive slippers hid her feet. Her hair was a mass of platinum, falling luxuriously over her shoulders. Like Tom's own, her eyes were the color of wet slates. Tom couldn't put words to the rest of her youthful face.

Propped up on her left arm, she had been reading a slim book when Tom first spied her. Now, with an insouciant gesture, she closed the book with a *clap*. It promptly vanished, and at the same time the music stopped. The woman stood.

Where she had lain, the grass — elsewhere so verdant as to look painted — was revealed to be even greener yet. The outline of her recumbent form enclosed a swatch of lawn that had been enhanced by her touch to a shade beyond naming, some part of the spectrum between green and indigo previously unrevealed. It was as if her lazy colored shadow remained behind, a reminder of her preternatural glory.

The woman opened her lips, and Tom noticed they were glossed silver. Then she spoke.

Her voice held secrets beyond what the music had so richly limned.

"Call me Mab —

"— Tom."

Book 2

4

At The Fork

> "And age is so much a part of, so inextricable from, the place where you were born or bred. So that away from home — space or time or experience away — you are always both older and eternally younger than yourself at the same time."
>
> — William Faulkner, "Mistral"

Orthodoxy, Tom later thought, is like pine-pitch. Once you touch it, no matter how hard you scrub, some always remains, sticky and annoying. Only rough abrasion finally wears it away. Along with a little skin.

Standing in the brake at the edge of the bower, his mind benumbed by music and hunger, visions and thirst, Tom had no conception of who this lounging woman could possibly be.

Until she spoke his name.

Then he knew.

Tom threw himself into the clearing, dropping to his bare knees on the exquisitely soft lawn. Clasping his hands in a prayerful attitude, he said:

"Holy Mary, Mother of God, forgive me my sins. I will call you Mab, or anything else you might bid me. Surely Thou hast Thy reasons. Let it never be recorded in Thy Son's book against my name that I dared question one syllable of Thy will. Although I have wondered at times exactly what motivated —"

Mab laughed. Her liquid trill, as perfectly natural as a nightingale's, and as brilliant, belled out to fill the glade. The massed flowers seemed to nod in appreciation of the joke she saw, although there was no breeze.

"Oh, Tom, what a goose you are! Stand up, and come to me here. You have much yet to learn, before you're ready for my purposes. I am not the Queen of Heaven, nor was I meant to be. You must get that straight from the start!"

Tom cut short his flood of apologies and beseechments. All the certainty which had momentarily possessed him vanished in a flash, to be replaced by total confusion. Where was it ever recorded that the Lord's Mother laughed in such a charming — one might almost say, pagan — manner? Further, Tom could not recall a previous instance of the Virgin ever insulting a worshipper by calling him "a goose." And what did she mean by "ready for my purposes?"

Utterly bewildered, Tom remained upon his knees. Mab, seeing he made no motion to rise, took the initiative. She glided across the green carpet and halted before Tom. Her scent — a melange of all the flowers in the grove, intensified by contact with her preternatural skin — came to Tom across the inches that separated them like the sound of a huntsman's horn to a fox: piercing, alarming, ecstatic unto death.

Tom could not bring himself to lift his gaze to meet hers. His world had dwindled to a horizon-filling swatch of green fabric, in which he swore he could trace each warp and weft thread.

Mab raised her hands into Tom's line of sight. The nail of each perfect finger was long and silver. All the hands Tom had seen in his life — save perhaps Natty Spurgeon's — had been seamed with work, the nails cracked and blunted.

Tom felt rather than saw Mab lay her hands upon his shoulders. Instantly, without even an eyeblink of transition, he was standing. But he had not willed it.

"There, that's more dignified, isn't it, Tom?" Mab asked.

Not wishing to stare rudely at this woman, Tom kept his eyes lowered, and merely nodded.

"Oh, no," Mab said next, with genuine concern. "You've hurt yourself."

Of a sudden, Tom felt something wet dripping down along his left jaw. He put a hand up to his face, and withdrew it all bloody. Apparently, when bursting through the brake, he had gouged himself on a branch.

"We can't have that," Mab said. Tom, reassured by her solicitous tone, dared to raise his eyes.

If possible, Mab was more beautiful up close than she had been across the glade. Like the blades of grass and the threads of her kirtle, Tom noticed, each platinum root of her hair seemed distinct and self-existent. It was as if she contained so much reality that each tiny portion of her — and whatever she graced — was endowed with scintillant power.

Meeting Tom's stare, Mab did the unexpected.

From between her parted silvered lips poked a pointy pink tongue as supple as a snake. With it she licked her right palm, like a cat. This moist palm she applied to Tom's wound.

Tom sensed the bleeding stop all at once.

Mab's palm came away clean, unmarred by blood or dirt.

"You're tired and hungry," Mab said, feigning not to notice Tom's amazement. "Come sit with me, and we'll refresh ourselves."

Tom let himself be led back to the slope where Mab had been resting. Gracefully, she folded her legs beneath herself, drawing Tom down too, as if by a string. They sat beside each other, a small space between, beneath the pergola of blossoms. Mab's robe formed a valley between the peaks of her knees.

"Water first, I think," she said.

Tom watched as Mab drew a hand across the grass between them.

A small pool formed in the hillside. It bubbled at its center like a spring, and in a second had overflowed, forming a rill down the grassy bank between Tom and Mab. Tom hastily withdrew his feet from its path.

"Drink deep, and wash your face," Mab commanded.

Tom needed little urging. He lowered himself toward the water.

For an instant, his reflection stopped him. In the pool he saw an unfamiliar face. Blackened with dirt and spotty stubble (except where Mab's hand had rested; that oval patch — her brand — was pink and smooth as a rosepetal), showing traces of anxiety and exhaustion, it reminded him of the uneasy countenance of his co-walker, or waff, on that night so long ago. The red and black roses that circled his face in the watery mirror disturbed him also, for reasons he could not name.

Shattering the image, he plunged willfully into the water, welcoming the coolness and vowing to be more attentive to the changes the Great Road and his other experiences were putting him through. It would never do to become so different from his own image of himself that he couldn't recognize his own reflection!

After scrubbing vigorously, he waited for the water to run clear, then drank long and deep. When he was finished, he looked up.

In Mab's lap was a hammered silver tray. It bore fruit

in exotic profusion. There were pomegranates red as rubies and apples green as spring. Pears as mellow-skinned as Oriental maidens nudged clusters of grapes as dusky as Nubian women. Oblate tangerines seemed ready to burst their rinds with juice. Plums like the eggs of some unlikely bird nestled next to fuzzy peaches.

"Something light, but filling," said Mab. "Try what you will, Tom."

Resisting the abrupt pangs of hunger that made his stomach growl, Tom reached tentatively toward the tray in Mab's lap. Selecting a peach, he bit hungrily into its pulp. Unbelievably sweet juices laved his palate, unlike anything he had ever experienced, and coated his throat like honey. He had never tasted anything so refreshing. Suddenly he could control himself no longer and wolfed the fruit down, tossing the pit over his shoulder. Other morsels equally good soon followed, until he could hold no more.

Rather chagrined at his unrestrained appetite, Tom regarded Mab. The water and food had relaxed him, restoring his old self. For the first time since he had fallen under the geas of harp, pipe and symphony, he felt competent and assured again. Whatever this woman was, Tom felt he could meet her as an equal.

Mab eyed Tom with an undisguised air of possessive humor. The nearly invisible smile that played about her moon-colored lips suddenly angered him.

"Who are you?" Tom demanded. "What's your interest in me?"

"You thought me Queen of Heaven," Mab reminded him.

Tom blushed.

Mab's smile became broader. "My title you perceived, but not my estate. Guess again, Tom."

Tom racked his brains. He knew Mab was no mortal queen. What was left?

Although it hurt to say it, Tom finally ventured another name. "Persephone?"

Mab's laughter was unbridled again. "And this is my six months aboveground, coincident with spring? No, Tom, I'm afraid not. Listen, I shan't tease you anymore. My realm is one you must have heard of. Faerie, mortals call it."

Tom had indeed heard of Faerie. But only in this wise:

The community Tom had grown up in was on intimate terms with supernatural beings of all stripes. Boggles and bogies, doonies and dunnies, feens and feeorin, grogans and gruagachs, noggles and nuckelavees, skrikers and spriggans, wilkies and wulvers. But all these beings were rather domestic creatures, residents of barns and hearths, lochs and swamps. They could be met with — luckily or unluckily — under mundane circumstances. There was nothing exotic about them, and their haunts were the very pastures and woods where Tom's folks grazed their cows and hunted their grouse.

Quite to the contrary, Tom had never met any inhab-

itant of Faerie, or any mortal who claimed to have visited that kingdom of uncertain qualities. It was no more
than a name to him, a term for a place beyond the
common fields mortals knew. He had no greater idea of
what life in Faerie was like than he had of court life in
Byzantium or Cathay, in Prester John's empire or the
Caliphate of Baghdad. If he had ever faintly imagined
that Faerie was what he was searching for — and he
didn't remember ever doing so — he would no more
have thought of going there than he would have seriously pondered a voyage to the moon.

Yet now, drinking in the exquisite beauty and organic
power of this woman seated so miraculously beside him,
an imperial force owing obvious allegiance to neither
heaven nor hell, Tom became instantly certain that
Faerie was what he had seen in the kirkyard — if only in
a partial glimpse — and what he had been looking for
ever since.

"What — what is —" Tom forced himself to calm
down, swallowing a huge lump in his throat. "What is
Faerie like?"

Hardly daring to hope her answer might confirm his
speculations, Tom waited breathlessly for Mab to reply.

Her first word nearly stopped his heart.

"Harmony," Mab said, "reigns in Faerie. A harmony
between the individual and the world. By this, Tom, I
mean a specific quality you must not mistake for the
eternal snooze of heaven. There is violence and pain in
Faerie, self-caused misery and rage, along with much

good cheer and happiness. But taken altogether, Faerie's harmony is not a thing of somnolence and quiet. Rather, it is a synchronization of the individual with the external empire of the senses."

Mab paused, then said, "Oh, drat these paltry words! Like tar, they blacken what they seek to preserve. Let me try again, Tom."

Mab took one of Tom's hands in hers. A surge of power shot up his arm, like lightning coursing through an iron rod, and Tom's mind felt like an uninhabited room, full of cobwebs, through which a cold wind had just blown.

"Faerie is a land without dichotomies. All the dualities you labor under here — man and beast, male and female, good and evil, self and other, even action and inaction — are subsumed in Faerie into a glorious whole. Whatever one does in Faerie is right, could happen no other way, granted the essential makeup of the individual who acts. In such a place, all doubts as to the rightness of one's life disappear, to be replaced by an exaltation of self."

Tom waited for Mab to continue, but she appeared to have exhausted the language's potential — or said as much as she wished. Her words, initially blazing in his head like levin across the night, gradually faded away, leaving only a faint afterglow of partial understanding.

"It sounds — it sounds like something I've dreamed of all my life," Tom said at last. "But I just don't know. It seems I can't be certain about anything anymore." Tom shook his head ruefully, like a dog with a tick it couldn't dislodge by scratching. "Once, I thought I knew what good and evil were. I wanted to discover a way between them, and it seemed I was on the trail of it. But along that trail, I ran into a few snares."

Mab inclined her head in an attentive way, and Tom was moved to pour out all the tribulations he had undergone so recently.

"So you see," he concluded, "the man whom I thought was my good friend — Natty — turned out to be a blackguard. And the other one — Nathan — whom I distrusted at first, had nothing at heart but my welfare. Although I nearly got killed that time too. If I don't understand the truth about good and evil, then how can I be sure my middle way — which is the same as Faerie, you claim — is even what I want?"

Mab nodded. "A good point, Tom." Elbow on thigh, she rested her perfect chin in one hand. Her eyes sparkled with an emotion Tom could not name, but which he suspected was uncomfortably close to what an alchemist felt regarding the base lead he proposed to convert to gold.

"What would you say to a further course of study, Tom? A closer look at good and evil, to help you decide? If you consent, after you finish I'll tell you more about Faerie — and you'll be ready to understand."

"Well, I suppose — That is —" Tom realized his vacillation was making him look like a coward and simpleton in front of this beautiful woman. He plunged headlong into acceptance.

"What I mean to say is, sure, I'll do it. If you think it'll help."

Mab clapped her hands in delight. "Wonderful! You won't regret it, Tom. But we've no need to rush right off. Let's rest a bit. Would you like to play a game I know?"

Having metaphorically thrown his dice, and being now suspended in that endless moment between toss and result, when all possibilities were equally likely, Tom felt curiously at ease, knowing nothing he could do at this moment would affect the outcome of his gamble. It was as if he were riding an oarless, rudderless craft through rocky rapids, and had to trust the blind kinetic forces of nature to see him through. The exultation almost made him drunk.

"Anything you say is fine — Mab. I'm good at games. Have you ever played at dambrod? I've a board right here . . ."

"An interesting game," Mab agreed. "But I've a better one. Observe."

A wave of her elegant hand across the water vanished that fountain. In its place appeared the game.

Studying it, Tom saw that the board was identical to that of draughts: sixty-four alternating red and black squares. The pieces, however, were another story. On the back rank, there were five different kinds: two tall central ones, flanked on either side by three others. The front rank consisted of eight identical pieces, making six kinds in all.

"Chess," Mab said. "The pieces are" — her finger

touched each one in turn — "Tower, Steed, Friar, Liege, Consort. In front, the Pikemen. They move thusly." An illustration followed. "The object is to capture your opponent's Liege, without losing your own. Do you think you can essay a game?"

Still feeling high, Tom said, "Who moves first?"

"Red. I'll palm a Pikeman of each color, and you pick a first."

Mab shuffled the red and black figures behind her back, offered outheld hands. Tom picked. Black.

Mab moved first: the Pikeman in front of her Consort's Friar ventured ahead one square. Tom, after some consideration, brought forth a frisky Steed.

The game was underway.

Tom found himself having to concentrate keenly on the board. No simple battle like dambrod was this. It seemed some stylized representation of life itself, endless plots and maneuverings, little victories and defeats scattered along the path to the larger goal. It took all his intellect to discern even the outlines of Mab's strategy.

The outcome was foredoomed. Although he held out valiantly, and not without a little flair, Tom eventually found his pieces reduced to a brace of Pikemen, a Friar, and of course, his Liege. Mab's crimson Consort raced down the board and soon she claimed checkmate. Tom resigned.

"A little lesson, Tom," she said without gloating. "Beware the Consort. The Liege is nothing, next to her."

"I'll remember," Tom promised.

The board joined the spring, the depleted tray of fruit and Mab's book in oblivion. Recalling the book, Tom, looking for a topic he could discourse knowingly on after his defeat, asked Mab what she had been reading when he first arrived.

"A book you can't know of," Mab replied rather off-puttingly.

Tom was annoyed by the curt reply. (It was amazing, the range of emotions he had experienced since encountering this woman. Veneration, fear, embarrassment, gratitude, friendship, anger — What next? he wondered.)

"I'm not illiterate, you know," Tom protested. "Look, do you know many who have read a book this big and important?"

Rummaging in his battered bag, Tom came up with his lone tome and held it out for Mab's inspection.

"A fine volume," Mab said placatingly. "Full of a real desire to understand. But it's rather long-winded, isn't it? And I think you'll agree that it conforms too closely to a view of life we both agree is incomplete."

Tom nodded reluctant agreement.

"Now the brief book I was reading — by a Frenchman named Arouet, who writes under a penname — is considerably deeper. I didn't mean you wouldn't like or understand it, Tom. Only that it wasn't available to you. Perhaps someday you'll get to read it. But not now."

Mab's tone left Tom no way to remain offended. He dismissed the matter from his mind, and waited for Mab's next suggestion.

Coming out of her fakir's posture in a fluid movement too quick for Tom to comprehend, Mab gained her feet. Tom followed suit, with only mortal swiftness.

"The heat of noon is on the wane," Mab said. "Time for us to be off."

These were the words Tom had been waiting for.

Yet a moment of bewilderment nailed Tom's eager feet to the ground.

"Where are we going?" he asked.

Nearly every other thing Tom did or said seemed to make Mab laugh. He wondered if it was entirely his fault, or if all mortals had this effect on the Faerie folk, or if Mab was just particularly risible. He suspected it was some combination of all three factors.

When Mab was finished enjoying his confusion, she replied, "Why, out to the Great Road, of course. Isn't that the path you chose to follow from the start?"

"Well, yes, I had thought to make my way back there eventually. Of course, I was enjoying my sojourn here in the forest so much — the trees and squirrels and what not — that I had hoped. . . I mean, I would never have met you if not for straying here. Not that I was lost or anything like that. Just idling by, that sort of thing . . ."

Mab's knowing grey eyes took in Tom's scratched calves and branch-lashed cheeks, a rip in his outsized shirt and grass-stains on his bare knees.

"It's a good thing you weren't lost," she said. "Men have wandered in these woods until they laid their bones down to bleach. Ancient forces still seek to ensnare hapless wanderers here."

Tom looked beyond the enchanted glade to the suddenly menacing trees beyond. A shiver ascended his spine with lizard's claws, despite the May sun. "How far is the Great Road?"

Mab contained any laughter, and Tom was grateful. "Only a short journey. Especially by the route I know."

Tom was about to say that he hoped Mab's route was an easy one — considering the delicacy of her footgear and the impenetrability of certain portions of the forest — when she startled him by shouting out two names.

"Endymion! Lug! To me at once!"

Twin thrashings sounded from among the trees beyond the green ambit, as if visitors had suddenly materialized in two separate spots, or had been waiting hidden throughout their interview. Tom didn't know in which direction to look. He decided to focus on the noisier of the two visitors, and turned his head just in time to see the arrival of Endymion.

A milk-white charger crashed through the brushy palisade with frightful snortings and tossings of its massive head. It galloped across the clearing toward Mab and Tom as if intending to trample them. It jingled as it came, the result of bells woven into its long mane and jangling brasses on its harness. Rooty gouts of turf were churned up by its weighty hooves, the fore ones shod in silver, the rear in gold.

Tom moved closer to Mab, and hoped to hell she had planned this.

The snowy horse bore down on them like an avalanche. Closer, closer . . . Tom felt he was going to vanish right up its dilated nostrils —

It stopped on a shilling, denying physics and affirming metaphysics.

Mab stroked the quivering flanks of the enormous steed as if it were a kitten. "Good horse, Endymion. Good horse. I want you to meet Tom."

Nervously advancing, Tom extended a shaky hand. The horse nuzzled it with its prehensile lips, and Tom was reassured.

"He's named Endymion," Mab explained, "since he's in love with me, and one of my avatars is Selene."

Tom nodded as if it were the most natural thing in the world, for a woman to reveal that one of her guises was a lunar goddess old as mankind.

Flickers teased a corner of his right eye. Tom realized that the other visitor must have arrived, and was standing behind him. He turned to confront this new member of their party.

No one was there.

But now there was darting movement in the corner of his left eye.

Tom spun like a top.

Nothing.

Something tapped his right shoulder.

Twisting, he knew already he was going to be too slow.

Empty air was all that greeted him.

A hand slapped the top of his head.

Tom reached up to grab the offending member, but it was gone. Instead, his shirt suddenly cinched his waist like Endymion's girth strap. He reached behind himself to find that the excess material of his borrowed garment had been knotted into a tight ball. At the edge of his vision, he thought to detect the shaking of something silently laughing.

Furious now, Tom whirled in a circle, desperate to lay his hands on this sprite. Naught availed. Every reaction of his was always too late to catch the offender.

Mab was laughing once more, too heartily to speak. At last she got herself under control. Gasping, she said, "All right, Lug. Stand still and behave yourself now. This is our new friend, Tom."

Tom came out of his final crouch and straightened, trying to regain his dignity before meeting this playful newcomer.

What he saw made him lose all concern with vanity.

A being only four feet tall stood before him. From head to foot, it was one vast improbability.

Blue spikes of hair grew above a furrowed brow and stopped short above warty jug ears. A single eye twice as big as a human's filled the space above a flat, splayed nose. Facial hair — also blue — covered a wide mouth and jaw. Below this was where the really impossible portion of the creature began.

From the ventral center of a heavily muscled torso shot a single arm and hand. Directly from the bottom of the trunk sprouted a single leg, thick as a tree, ending in a broad foot. The creature was endowed with a coat of blue quills halfway between feathers and hair. Its sex, if any, was concealed where thigh joined torso.

Tom was poleaxed. His mind spun like a waterwheel at floodtime, threatening to tear itself loose from its moorings. It wasn't the creature in and of itself that was so upsetting.

It was that Tom had seen it before.

A stormy night, three knocks, two flashes of lightning, and an accustomed life was shattered.

When Tom found his voice, it was as glacial as a boreal wind.

"Mab, I have to know something before we take a single step together. Where were you and Lug roughly a month ago?"

Tom waited like a stock, dreading the answer.

Mab's face was a model of honest concern. She regarded Tom deeply before she spoke.

"If it truly matters to you, Tom, I'll be happy to tell you. Lug and I were both in Faerie. In fact, this is our first trip out in over a year."

Mab took Tom's hand as a token of her earnestness. He steeled himself against the raw power of her being, but she seemed disinclined to use it at this crucial juncture, relying instead on words alone.

"That's the truth, Tom. I wouldn't lie to you. Remember that, whatever happens."

Tom wagged his head, not understanding anything. He felt simultaneously a thousand years old and innocent as a babe. "I just don't get it," he said.

"Tell me what's bothering you, Tom. Perhaps I can explain."

Slowly at first, Tom detailed how his fetch had visited him, along with Lug, whose actual name had even been used, and the inexplicable events that had quickly followed.

Reassuringly, after Tom was done, Mab said, "Part of the mystery is easily solved, Tom. The simple fact is that Lug is not unique."

Tom looked at the creature and shuddered. A whole race of these?

"Lug," Mab continued, "belongs to that tribe called fachans. His kind seldom ventures far from Faerie, which is why you're not familiar with him. As for his name, Lug is a common appellation among fachans. Lug, how many others do you know with your name?"

Lug, grinning beneath his blue beard, held up five fingers.

"Of course, five is as high as Lug can count. But he means to indicate a larger number than five, by far. So you see, Tom, that much is susceptible to unriddling. As for your co-walker — well, it's common knowledge that waffs are usually a sign of impending death for those they mimic. But you've outlived any such short-term prophecy by now. I wouldn't worry about it."

Tom pondered his options. As usual in this world, it seemed he had only two. He could believe Mab, or he could doubt her. In the first case, all was well. In the second, he must have nothing to do with her, on the off-chance that she was somehow connected with that night of terror that had resulted in the death of Tom's beloved mother. His course of action rested entirely on how much he trusted her.

He studied her beautiful features for signs of treachery. All he saw was a knowledge and morality as far beyond his as his code transcended that of a savage, storm-driven inhabitant of the Outer Hebrides.

"I trust you," Tom finally said, knowing that his choices this time had really numbered only one.

Mab's smile was reward enough for Tom's faith.

"Shake hands with Lug, Tom, and you'll find you have a firm friend."

Tom lifted his hand. Lug hopped forward with the power, precision and dexterity that had allowed him to elude Tom. They shook.

"Lug says he's glad to meet you," Mab offered. "The fachans have no powers of speech, but I can interpret his expressions."

"Glad to know you too, Lug," Tom said, willing to forgive the fachan's tricks, in the interest of future harmony.

Mab snatched Endymion's bridle with a decisive gesture. "Now, the day is slipping out from under us. We must hie away!"

Out of nowhere, a velvet green mantle, fastened with a silver chain, appeared around Mab's shoulders. Setting one green-shod foot into a stirrup, Mab vaulted into Endymion's saddle. Her gown hiked up high on her legs, which Tom saw were whiter than birch saplings and incomparably more beautiful. From finely boned ankles to the thighs that clutched Endymion, they sent a peculiar thrill through Tom, at once enthralling and scaring him. On the whole, he decided, he rather envied Endymion.

Mab appeared not to notice the effect she had on Tom. She contemplated the wall of the forest instead. Tom wondered if she were going to charge in, replaying Endymion's entrance in reverse.

Such was not what Mab had in mind. She waved her arm in a gentle arc, and Tom saw the dense barrier to their departure disappear. At the spot Mab had picked, a passage opened, cutting into the dense forest like a hole poked through butter.

Mab clucked to Endymion, who broke into a gentle walk. Tom found he could easily keep pace with the horse and rider. Lug, of course, had no trouble at all.

They stopped by the hill, so that Tom could retrieve satchel and staff, and then they entered the foliage-roofed tunnel.

The glade dwindling behind him seemed the closest thing to home Tom had known in a long time, although he had spent only part of a morning and afternoon there. He felt sad to depart, knowing he would never see it again.

In the tunnel, Tom noticed that they trod a carpet of white hawthorn flowers.

But there was not a single hawthorn tree to be seen.

After some time spent in silent movement, they reached the tunnel's far end and stepped out upon the Great Road. Tom turned for one last look backward.

The solid forest presented its enigmatic face. No sign of their arbor-like passage remained.

Mab and Lug were already moving away down the Road. Tom hastened after them.

When he came alongside Endymion, he realized that if he kept directly abreast of the seated Mab, he would be in a distinctly embarrassing position only a few inches away from her bare leg, his head on a level with her saddle. Hurriedly, he jogged a couple of steps ahead, and took up with Endymion instead. He held the horse's halter lightly, relishing the comforting reality of leather and horseflesh against his hand. He felt less like a Peeping Tom with his back to Mab. And he could even pretend that he was the head of this party, leading his fair lady on her palfrey.

Neither Mab nor Endymion disabused Tom of this conceit, nor did they object to his guidance. So in this fashion, Lug hopping circles around them like an autonomous champagne cork, they made their way down the

Great Road, the sunlight cascading like a dry golden waterfall around them.

The next few hours passed without conversation. Tom's thoughts were relatively unanxious, as he became caught up in the pace and rhythm of walking. The sun soothed him, as did the presence of his companions. Even the uncanny Lug was becoming something of an accepted fact of life. Tom's concerns narrowed down to his next stride, and the brasses jangling against Endymion's muzzle. The image engraved on those ornaments was a thistle, and Tom thought it a fit signature for Mab, who was also beautiful but prickly.

Mab's quiet matched his own, although what her thoughts were — whether they would even be comprehensible to him — he could not say.

At last Tom remembered that Mab had left one question of his unanswered, back in the glade. He wondered if she had done so deliberately. Perhaps if he asked, again — ? There was no harm in trying, he decided. And also, without the distraction of Mab's face before him, he might be able to push her more keenly.

"Mab?" Tom began.

"Yes?"

"Why are you helping me? What am I to you? Surely the Queen of Faerie has more important matters to attend to."

"You must not try to limit or predict me, Tom," Mab said somewhat formally. "My impulses and concerns are not cut with the same template as yours. I do as I will, and that is the whole of the laws that bind me. Is that clear?"

Abashed, Tom only bobbed his head.

Her voice falling into a sweeter cadence, Mab continued. "Let's just say, Tom, that I always take an interest in young men such as yourself. Over the years — more years than you might imagine — I have helped a number of them. And I have always been amply rewarded."

Tom tried to imagine what he might have that this Queen could want. But his mind didn't stretch that far yet. Reference to his predecessors filled him with trepidation also. Where were they now?

Further miles in silence eroded. Then Tom thought of something else. As neutrally as possible, he said:

"Is there a King of Faerie, Mab?"

"There is a moon, and there is also a sun," Mab replied. "But one does not always see them in the sky together."

That was a lot to chew on. Tom didn't think his brain could handle any more such answers. He would have liked to know exactly where they were going, but he held his tongue.

Eventually the Great Road shed the forest like a snake crawling out of its skin. The countryside around them was now comprised of open meadows, covered with heather, which stretched away to distant, haze-shrouded hills. A change in the road occurred at this point. From trampled dirt, it became paved with stones, as when Natty and Tom had walked it through the marshlands. Only this time the stones were different from the earlier dun-colored cobbles. Rose and ebony granite, full of sparkling mica flakes that caught the fading sunlight, was laid chessboard-fashion. Tom had a sudden flash of dizziness, and his identity seemed to slip away. Of a sudden, he felt himself to be a Pikeman leading his Consort on her Steed, across a geometric world, where his every move was constrained by rules he could not violate.

The spell passed, and he knew himself again to be Thomas Rhymer, master of whatever small destiny he might possess.

Dusk was gathering now, like the folds of a black mantle. Behind the hills, the sinking sun exhaled clouds of red. The Road stretched away before them, and Tom wondered when they would stop for the night.

Raising his head from contemplation of the checkered Road, Tom got a surprise. Two tiny figures occupied the center of the Road, almost at the limits of Tom's vision at this twilit hour. One seemed to be dressed entirely in red, the other in black.

Looking over their shoulders, the two figures spotted Tom and Mab at the same time. They halted, and, apparently, began to argue. The red one tried to run away, but the black one caught him. Then they started to fight.

Tom broke into a run, certain of whom they had stumbled upon. Mab cantered after, saving any questions about Tom's precipitous behavior for later.

Tom covered the quarter-mile in well under a minute.

Even before he reached the figures rolling around on the pavement, he had had his suspicions confirmed.

His legs shaking, striving for breath, Tom stood above the struggling pair. Lug and Mab, who could have easily won the race, pulled up a few seconds after. Lug began to hop gleefully around the tussling couple.

Nathan left off fighting first. He extricated himself from the complicated hold the sinuous Natty had wrapped around him and stood. He picked up his floppy black hat from the dust and began to brush it off.

Natty had gained his pantherine feet by this time too. With economical gestures he flicked the powder of the Road from his scarlet suit.

Tom studied the two men, who had played such a subjectively large part in his life.

Nathan's hat was missing a piece of its brim, as if someone had taken a bite from it. He smelled of smoke, and a charcoal smear crossed one gaunt cheek. Natty's dapper clothing had undergone even greater alterations than Shiverick's coarse outfit. He had lost his bright scarf. One shirtsleeve was barely attached at the shoulder. The other had a long rip up its length. His crimson trousers were covered with dried encrustations, as if he had landed in a dungheap. Still he retained his sardonic expression, as if holding the world by the tail.

Tom, breathing less rapidly now, opened his mouth to unleash a pack of recriminations. What a score he had to settle with these two! But before the first verbal hound could escape to savage its intended targets, Natty had leapt into the breech.

"Tom, I can die at last! My life is complete, now that we are reunited! I've been searching for you ever since that unseemly fracas in Burdock's. I was knocked unconscious, did you know? When I came to, forgotten in a shadowy corner of the inn, everyone was gone! Hunting throughout the town for you, I was beset by a mob of hooligans who were chasing this fellow beside me, who claims to be a snake-oil salesman of some sort. Nahum Silverprick, he calls himself, I believe."

Nathan shook his morose head, as if to say, *Listen to this scoundrel.*

"In any case," Natty went on, "the vigilantes mistook me for someone else, against whom they had a grudge, and I was forced to flee for my life. Nahum and I at last escaped that village of madmen, and have been roving ever since, always on the alert for your scent. Why, when I saw you just now I was so overjoyed that I flung up my arms, accidentally striking Silverprick here, who naturally misconstrued my enthusiasm and struck back."

"That's a lie," Nathan mournfully intoned. "When he saw you, Spurgeon advised me to run, saying you were brigands, intent on cutting our purses and throats. Had I not put the fear of the Lord into him, he would be long gone by now."

Natty clicked his tongue in indignation. Choosing not deny Nathan's charge, he instead turned his attention to Mab. His vulpine eye ran up her shapely legs, stopping to admire the silver chain at her throat, and finally settled on her face.

"Did I mention yet, good Lady, that this boy is like a son to me?"

"I can see what you feel," Mab said with a chilling smile.

Disconcerted for the first time since Tom had met him, Natty looked away and concerned himself with sartorial matters.

Tom found he had no heart any longer to chastise these two. Whatever they had done to him, with good will or bad, he had first willingly put himself into their hands. He instantly resolved to consider all accounts clean, and begin their relationship anew.

"Well, I'm happy to meet up with both of you again," Tom said. "You mean something to me that I wouldn't care to lose. You're welcome to walk with us — that is, if Mab consents." Tom looked up to Mab, who regally said, "You've accepted *my* friends so graciously, Tom, I'd be a churl to spurn *yours*. Let them come with us for as far as they want."

At the mention of Mab's friends, the two men seemed to notice Lug for the first time. After some initial startlement, both Natty and Nathan appeared to accept the fachan, Natty with the indifference of one who accounted all other creatures, mortal or Faerie, inferior to himself, and Nathan with the superiority of those *with* souls over those *without*.

While they talked, darkness had overtaken them. Above, stars ate holes in the cloth of the sky, like white-hot coals scattered on wool, A nightbreeze sprang up, blowing from the far hills and across the meadows, carrying the scents of moist earth and growing things.

"I propose we shelter among the trees, my friends," Natty said. "Out on this plain, we present an easy target for any gruesome night-stalker who desires a midnight snack."

Here Natty eyed Lug, as if he were a quisling in their camp.

Hesitant to take his first backwards step along his chosen route, Tom was about to object — although he had no alternative — when Mab spoke.

"Not at all necessary, good people. Just follow me."

She turned Endymion off to the right, and moved a few feet onto the heather. The others followed.

Clustered around Mab, they awaited her next action.

Her hand came up from the saddle's pommel and pointed to a spot a few feet beyond them. A silver flame blossomed where she bid. She whipped her arm up in a half-circle, and an argent rod was extruded from the spot, described an arc above them, and anchored itself where it met the earth again.

In seconds, after a series of subsequent gestures, the party was enclosed in a lambent silver birdcage.

Mab dismounted. "Don't touch the bars," she warned unnecessarily.

No one dared ask why.

Mab provided more fruit for their supper. (Tom watched Lug's manner of eating with fascination. He had never seen a hand and mouth so coordinated.) When they had sated themselves, they lay down to sleep.

Natty was on one side of Tom, and Nathan on the other. Soon the preacher was making noises like an industrious sawyer. Even cushioned by the scented heather, however, Tom found it harder to fall asleep, and turned uneasily over to see Natty's cage-lit eyes studying him.

"You travel with powerful company now, my boy," Natty whispered. "Do you suppose your pretty wench might magic me a new set of clothes? I am exceedingly partial to fine linens and silk."

"Why don't you ask her?" Tom countered.

Natty smiled rather more weakly than was his wont, and turned over without making an answer.

Silently laughing — in what was positively a Mab-like way — Tom fell asleep.

In the morning, when the mortals awoke, they found the cage gone and breakfast awaiting: a flagon of water and more fruit.

Natty grumbled something about needing red meat and beer, but ate more than his share of peaches and apricots. In this he was balanced by Nathan, who ate sparingly, as if to mortify the flesh.

Soon they were back on the Great Road, moving as Mab directed.

Late afternoon found them at the first branching of their way.

The Road at this point became a Y. The bicolored paving split, forming a black road and a red one. The red one angled off to the left, the black to the right. The land here was rather low and swampy on all sides, forming a treacherous, despondent-looking slough. But in the crotch of the Y, Tom thought to detect a difference in the terrain. There, the marshy ground seemed insubstantial, a mirage, like a veil across *terra incognita*.

"Natty," Tom asked, "does the ground straight ahead seem queer to you?"

Natty denied he saw anything out of the ordinary.

When Nathan was asked, he too vouchsafed the same opinion. Just plain marsh, that's all it was.

Tom was about to ask Mab, but she was staring up at the sky, at nothing in particular, and he hesitated to interrupt her.

When she again paid them any heed, her words drove everything else from Tom's mind.

"This is where we must part."

5
The Scarlet Empire

"Don't let it bring you down,
"It's only castles burning . . ."

— Neil Young,
"Don't Let It Bring You Down"

The westering sun behind Mab put Tom in her shadow. A corona around her dazzled his eyes. Backlit, she and Endymion looked like silhouettes cut from one of the black crystal spheres that held the sun and planets and stars in their orbits. Although he had known her for only a little more than a day, Tom realized that he could not imagine going on without her. A future empty of her magnificent presence seemed an intolerable prison sentence, without chance of pardon. What would he do with his life, lacking Mab as a token of the possible attainment of Faerie, that realm that now represented to him all he sought?

"You can't —" Tom began to protest.

Mab's transmogrification cut him off.

Her image seemed to swell twice lifesize, till she became a giantess astride a mountainous beast. In the blackness of her form, moon-colored pools opened where one would expect eyes and mouth, Endymion's eyes and nostrils flared silver also. The two of them seemed wraiths from the cold and silent ether between earth and moon.

Tom flung up a hand before his eyes, cowed and trembling. "*Ahhh*!" he said, and hunched away.

Nathan and Natty soon were by his side, solicitous and seeking to ascertain what was wrong.

"What ails you, lad?" Nathan asked.

"It's a fit brought on by lack of real sustenance," Natty claimed. "Give him some beer, and he'll come straight around."

Tom's vision danced with motes of silver against a nigrescent backdrop. He weakly took his hands away from his blasted eyes and straightened. Gradually they began to clear. He regarded the two men beside him for a moment, before signalling with a feeble wave that he was all right.

Then, because he had to, he looked at Mab.

The sun had dropped further while Tom underwent his seizure, and now no longer lit Mab in the same fashion. Endymion's hooves clattered on the stones, and he and Mab moved a few feet, altering their relation to the red orb even more. They looked again as of old, no more wraithlike than Tom himself. And from the calm expressions his companions exhibited, Tom knew they had experienced nothing of Mab's transformation.

Mab's face, though human, was stern. "Do not ever say I cannot do a thing," she coolly reprimanded.

"I won't," Tom replied.

Mab gauged the depth of his pledge and, apparently satisfied, continued in a milder tone.

"We do not part forever here, Tom. I am sending you on alone to learn that which we discussed yesterday. You recall our conversation, I am sure. The first half of your education lies ahead of you, down the red branch of the Great Road. Red first — on a whim of mine, and since red was the victor in our game of chess.

"I have sent messengers ahead of you, to the ruler of the land you are about to visit. You are assured of at least a diplomatically cordial reception, although I caution you to be always on your guard in this man's empire. His impulses are unpredictable, and might overmaster his awe of me — especially the longer you remain with him."

Tom found it hard to believe that anyone might contravene Mab's expressed wishes.

"That is why I am sending Lug with you," added Mab.

At the mention of his name, the fachan hopped with excitement in a series of figure eights that enclosed Mab and Endymion in one loop, and Tom, Natty and Nathan in the other.

"Through Lug, I will be able to witness what befalls you. He will also be your means of returning instantly to me, should the need arise. Simply speak my name to him with a request to join me, and we will be reunited."

Lug thumped himself on his — chest? — as if to indicate that Tom could rely on him.

"As for your friends," Mab said, "they may accompany you — in which case they will enjoy the same protection as yourself — or they may go their own way, back to Ercildoune, or down the black Road. It is entirely up to them."

Presented with this choice, Nathan and Natty became pensive. Nathan began to finger the hairy mole projecting from his eyebrow like a boulder from a field. Natty rested a delicate digit against the flank of his nose. At the same time, Tom found himself unconsciously touching the bald patch on his jaw that Mab's palm had left. With a start, he realized that the three of them must look like students at a school for mimes, the day's lesson being *Conveying Deep Thoughts.*

Tom dropped his hand in embarrassment, and spoke to cover his consternation. "I'd welcome your company, friends."

Nathan left off stroking his mole and said, "Perhaps the inhabitants of this land will respond favorably to my ministry. I believe I will come with you, Tom."

"Red is a propitious color for me," Natty declaimed. "And the notion of travelling under the patronage of so resplendent a lady as Tom's appeals to me. May I men-

tion, dear sovereign, in future social encounters, that I
am one of Mab's favorites?"

"You may do no such thing," Mab said.

Natty seemed only slightly disappointed, as if he had
not really expected permission, but had been compelled
to try for it by his overweening ambition.

"All is settled, then," Mab said. "I suggest you start
out at once. The land becomes firmer and dryer not far
from here, and you will be able to camp for the night."

Tom's scrip, strung over his shoulder, suddenly jerked
him down, heavy as a pannier filled with marketplace
goods.

"Suitable provisions to see you through the next day
are in your wallet, Tom. Farewell, Master Rhymer. Keep
your wits about you, and return to me when you feel you
have seen enough."

Mab swung Endymion's head about, presenting
them with the unedifying spectacle of the horse's white
hindquarters and thick tail, and began to trot away,
back down the Great Road. The four companions
watched her until she was out of sight in the gloam-
ing.

As she disappeared, Tom swore he heard faint supernal strains of harp and pipe and symphony.

Tom ended the silence. "Well, I suppose we must get
going, friends." He went to clap a hand on Lug's shoulder, as a gesture of solidarity, but stopped when he realized that the fachan, strictly speaking, did not possess a
shoulder, his blue-quilled torso narrowing abruptly from

the neck down. He contented himself with shaking Lug's hand once more.

Gripping his trusty walking stick firmly, Tom set off down the red branch, Natty and Nathan close behind.

An hour's subsequent walking brought them — as Mab had promised — to terrain that was suitable for passing the night; although, as Natty endlessly complained, it was exceedingly stony and hard, unlike last night's heather mattress.

Although there were no trees in sight, they managed to have a fire. Nathan, utilizing the last of the twilight, came upon a dry streambed not far from the Road, which was littered with driftwood that blazed admirably when the sparks from Tom's flint finally caught. Once settled around the comforting fire, Natty chafed his hands together with eagerness.

"It is my opinion," he said, "that Tom's lady took my culinary suggestions to heart, and amended our fare to include richer stuffs. Let's fall to, Tom!"

Opening his wallet, Tom reached within, severally withdrawing a dozen apples, four loaves of bread and two condensation-slick flagons of water.

"*Faugh*!" Natty spat. "Does this harlot fancy herself Eve, and us her Adams? Inanition will soon have us lying by the roadside, unable to walk. Mark my words!"

"Don't talk about Mab that way," Tom admonished severely. "If you don't like what she provided, you can go hungry."

Natty said nothing, but grabbed three apples and a

loaf and sullenly supped. When passed a flask, he wrinkled his nose, but drank more than half.

After supper, immensely tired from the day's journey and anticipating tomorrow's, beside the crackling flames, the travellers curled themselves up and went quickly to sleep.

The morning dawned in a strange fashion. The sky shed its coat of darkness reluctantly, as if ashamed to reveal the sickly pallor beneath. In place of yesterday's heavens of bright blue, the night gradually gave way to a canopy of oily, greasy grey, like clotted cream contaminated with a surface mold. This ominous sky swirled, as if agitated by the wings of squamous beasts below the horizon.

Looking ahead in their direction of travel, Tom saw that the sky was tinged with a band of burgundy color far away. No obvious cause for either the condition of the immediate heavens or the stripe of distant color was apparent.

Although uneasy, none of the three men commented on the sky, all preferring to believe it was merely a temporary disturbance of the atmosphere that would vanish in time. Lug, of course, could voice no opinion whatsoever, but he too seemed disturbed.

Deciding to save the remains of their supper to eat at midday, they left behind their camp, breaking their fast with water alone.

Only a few desultory words were exchanged during their entire morning's walk. Nothing about their environment conduced them to talk. As the miles piled up behind them, the wine-colored portion of the sky grew larger and larger, until it eventually stretched across half the celestial hemisphere, and seemed to be the lid of a dish that was sliding up to enclose them. Tom came to feel that they stood still, and that only this crimson cover was moving.

The moment arrived when they stood directly under the terminator of the red sky. To one side, the slimy heavens of the morning roiled, smoky and curdled. On the other, a scarlet fog diffused a sourceless incarnadined light. On neither side was the sun visible as a discrete thing. The interface of the two skies was impossibly solid, no mixing of the two media taking place.

Feeling responsible for their welfare and spirits, Tom sought to explain away the situation.

"There must be a forest fire somewhere," he said. "That would explain the smoke and glare."

Both Nathan and Natty stared at Tom as if he were a lunatic who had just proposed that men and apes were related, since they looked so much alike.

"Have you ever seen," Nathan asked, "a fire that could cause such a sky as this?"

"Let's have lunch," Tom replied.

After eating rather absentmindedly, Tom and the others moved on, now entirely beneath the red heavens. From this new vantage, it seemed that the dwindling grey sky behind them was the part that moved, a curtain pulled back to reveal the abominable.

Beneath their feet, the paving stones of the red branch seemed to acquire a new luster, as if gigantic snails had passed over them. The surrounding lands, friable earth devoid of vegetation and full of boulders, borrowed a somber hue from the bloody sky.

When the last grey had disappeared from behind them, Tom noticed two things.

First, it was becoming unseasonably warm. Perhaps his speculation about the fire had not been so far off the mark. The air was taking on a desiccated, moistureless quality. Tom associated this parched air with his one experience of the rooms attached to the church at Ercildoune, wherein the priest lived. He had had to visit the man when Harl Rhymer, Tom's father, had lain dying. Although it was only early October, a huge fire had been roaring in the priest's hearth as he stuffed himself with a roast goose tithed to him. Standing meekly, waiting for the fat priest to finish before he would come to shrive Tom's father, the boy had nearly fainted.

Now he felt the same way, as sweat began to bead his brow.

The second anomaly was Natty. He was reacting differently to this strange land than Nathan, Lug and Tom. Whereas the latter three were dragging their feet, Natty's walk was becoming more jaunty, his visage more wily and feral. The heat and somber landscape seemed to agree with him, feeding him with invisible currents of strength.

"Hop sprightly, my horrid boggle," Natty gleefully

addressed Lug. "Tom, Silverprick, pick up the pace. I believe we will soon be reaching the court of the mysterious Liege Mab has commended us to. No doubt we will be made much of, and I, for one, can hardly wait. A perfumed bath, a new outfit, and some real food are among the most basic of my requirements."

No one made a response. Natty, unabashed, began to whistle. Tom recognized the tune as a bawdy ditty known as "The Reluctant Virgin."

As if Natty's windy prophecies had suddenly become self-fulfilling, a sprawling mass of hovels became apparent ahead, after half an hour's progress through the tortured land. Stretching away to either side of the Road like a trash-heap, the low, shabby structures, pieced together from unidentifiable flotsom and jetsam, appeared to be the detritus left after some huge flood. Although it was hard to tell at this distance, the ramshackle village seemed to be threaded with noisome alleys. The whole assemblage had the air of cowering under the hematic sky, like a cur often whipped.

"Aha," Natty exclaimed, "these must be the slums clustering about the elegant grounds of the lord's estate. Let's get through them quickly, so we can gain admission to the manse."

Natty's glee and vigor were exhausting to contemplate, let alone match, and he began to forge ahead of the others.

Thus he was the first to meet Gorget.

From behind a huge stone shaped roughly like a cow's skull that lay beside the road boomed a *basso profundo* voice, deeper even than Nathan's.

"Halt," said the voice. "That is, if you would, please."

The party stopped, Natty separated by a few feet from the rest. They waited nervously for whoever had accosted them to make himself known. A few tense seconds passed before the sentry emerged.

A glossy red beetle big as a prize porker, its pincers waving, scuttled from behind the rock. Seated atop its back was a trollish mannikin, bald as a turnip, about three feet tall, with coppery skin.

Naked save for a twisted cloth wrapped around his loins and knotted on both sides of his waist, the mannikin was a creature so heavily muscled as to appear almost deformed. It appeared that years of constant work had endowed him with a physique Atlas might have admired. By comparison with the rest of his body, his face seemed unformed, a chubby, babyish visage. His ears were pointed, with tufts of wire-like hair at the tips.

"In the name of the Bastard King," the dwarf boomed, "I must ask your names before you go any further."

The title of the mannikin's lord sent a chill through Tom, although he could not have said why.

As if regretting the need for such brusqueness, the dwarf lowered his voice and confidentially said, by way of apology, "Mine's Gorget, by the way."

Natty — who seemed to be assuming the role of leader — recovered first, and spoke up.

"You confront the redoubtable Natty Spurgeon, sir, statesman and envoy extraordinary from the realms of day. The youth behind me is Thomas Rhymer, bard and poet to the lost kings of Atlantis. The monoped sports the sobriquet of Lug. And that gloomy funeral bird is called —"

"Nathan Shiverick," said the preacher, before Natty could mangle his name.

"Wonderful," said Gorget with a smile. "You're just the people we were expecting. I'm so glad I didn't have to strangle you all. Now if you'll just follow me, I'll put you up at my home overnight. By noon tomorrow, you'll be received by the Bastard King himself."

"Your offer of an intermediate roof," said Natty, with a deprecatory air, "is most welcome. However, could we not bypass your doubtlessly charming domicile, and proceed directly to the King's?"

"I don't think," said Gorget, "that you realize how far you have yet to go. Unless you're all more energetic than you look, I doubt if you could make it without a rest."

"That brings up a critical point," Natty said, straining up on tiptoe to look over Gorget. "I see no spires or machicolations of your lord's castle. Exactly how many miles ahead does it lie?"

"Less than one, as a stone drops," Gorget said.

"Ridiculous!" Natty said.

Gorget cringed, as if he were about to be struck. Tom noticed for the first time that his chest — and probably his back as well — was criss-crossed with welts and weals, some fresh, some healed.

"I beg your pardon, Master Spurgeon," the dwarf said, "but I only spoke the truth.

"You see — the castle's straight down."

Tom had been right about Gorget's back.

Wending his way among the filthy, stinking, claustrophobic streets of Gorget's home town, Tom consoled himself with the accuracy of his supposition.

It was really the only thing he could feel perversely satisfied about.

On the way to the hovels, trudging tiredly over the slick red cobbles of the Road, following behind the dwarf on his scurrying beetle, Tom had had plenty of time to study the muscle-slabbed shoulders of the mannikin. They were a welter of old scars and virginal gashes, as if someone had played innumerable games of oughts and crosses on his back with a lash.

Feeling sorrow, pity and not a little rage, Tom wondered what he and his friends were getting themselves into.

When Gorget had indicated that the four travellers should follow him, Tom had exerted his last few ounces of initiative and moved to the head of the file, displacing Natty as leader. Tom was determined to assert himself before they arrived among the other inhabitants of this vast wasteland. After all, he thought, who the hell's quest was this anyway — his or Natty's?

Natty had taken second place without grumbles or protests. He exuded the calm confidence of a runner who realized that his opponents, however distant now, would tire long before the final lap, leaving the victory to him. His carroty crop of hair, which Tom had once mistaken for a flower, now bore no resemblance to a plant, but seemed rather to mimic the brooding conflagration of the sky, flickering flames crowning his animated features.

Nathan and Lug had brought up the rear of the procession. The preacher had formed something of a special bond with the fachan, perhaps regarding him as a unique test of his persuasive powers. Tom could imagine Nathan touring the provinces with Lug, using him as a bizarre testimonial to the ineffable powers of Scripture.

Suddenly halting among the ordure and slops of the stenchy alley which the party wearily traversed, as if in a waking dream, Gorget swivelled atop his carapaced mount.

"Welcome to my home," Gorget said.

Tom raised his eyes from the mire in which his shoes were sunk to the ankles. He studied the building beside which they had paused.

Gorget's house had apparently been assembled by a team of feeble-minded drunkards in the middle of the night during a tumultuous storm. The lower portion of it was comprised of several courses of mortarless, unfinished stone. The upper half was a loose compilation of elephantine bones, petrified treelimbs, tatters of canvaslike cloth, insectoid scales big as shields, and rotten, fusty straw. The house differed from its neighbors only in the way one crazyquilt differed from another, and Tom could not imagine how Gorget had ever brought them through the directionless warren to this one particular shack.

Nimbly dismounting, Gorget loosely fastened his beetle's bridle to a projecting spar. He moved to a flap that hung raggedly and pulled it back to disclose an asymmetrical gap in the streetside wall.

"Enter, enter, don't be shy. My home is yours," Gorget said with immense hospitality.

Not seeing much difference between staying out in the street and partaking of Gorget's shelter, Tom stumbled through the door, followed by his friends and host.

Once inside, Tom was knocked to the ground by a half a dozen hurtling forms.

"Children, children!" Gorget shouted. "Where's your manners? This is no rough-and-tumble playmate of yours, but one of our distinguished visitors from the outside world. Let him stand!"

Gorget, through buffetings and cuffings, removed his rambunctious brood from Tom's recumbent body. Throughout the assault, Tom had remained motionless, too tired to resist. When uncovered, Tom was helped to his feet by Gorget and Nathan. They brushed him off and ascertained that he had suffered no injuries. Finally, Tom was able to look around.

The interior of Gorget's house was surprisingly clean. The floor was of packed earth, with no offal about. (The rubbish was obviously all out in the street.) There was no furniture, but some battered iron pots were stacked neatly in one corner, next to a ring of stones that contained a flickering blaze, which vented its smoke through the gaping roof. A nearby barrel held water with a scrim of algae atop it, and another vessel held coarse meal. The heat and dryness of the scarlet land was evidently unvarying, obviating the need for blankets or a weather-tight roof. Thanks to the sieve of a roof, the hut was almost as light inside as the gloomy land ever got.

Gorget moved to stand proudly beside his children, and a female of his kind. The female troll was as massively built as her mate, with thick-nippled breasts like beehive-crowned knolls. Hairless, she too wore only a loin-wrap.

With an arm around her, Gorget said, "My wife, Glimmerglitch. And the kids — our latest litter — are Gog, Gorget Junior, Geep, Grimly, Gaslark and Gorm."

Tom bowed politely to the self-similar imps who had so recently mistaken him for one of those greased poles at a festival which all comers are invited to try and climb.

"What's for dinner, Glim?" Gorget asked with a sly wink at his guests, as if to caution them to pay particular attention to his wife's answer.

"Cactus steaks and baked stuffed toadstools," Glimmerglitch replied.

Gorget slapped one meaty thigh, wordlessly proclaiming his satisfaction with his wife's menu. He directed his guests' appreciation of her abilities with much rolling of his big eyes and assorted gesticulations.

Glimmerglitch slipped away to the fire to begin the actual meal so fully enjoyed already by Gorget in his imagination. Meanwhile, Gorget sought to induce his children to perform any number of tricks for the visitors, such as handstands, backflips and counting from one to ten without bypassing any of the more confusing numbers.

After an interval, supper was announced. The family and the journeyers squatted perforce around the firestones.

Glimmerglitch doled out the food on flat sheets of shale, and, sans utensils, all the trolls began hungrily to eat.

Natty opened his mouth as if to carp and snipe at the fare, but Tom gave him such a scathing stare that he kept all comments to himself. Reluctantly, Natty too ate, as did the famished Tom and Lug. The cadaverous Nathan partook of his usual minuscule portion. The food was washed down with mouthfuls of thick water, taken from a common dipper.

When the meal was over, the children retreated to the far side of the hovel for sleep, as did Lug, whose enjoyment of what was, for him, literally "shuteye" had already been remarked on by his comrades earlier. The adults stayed up for a while, talking.

"Could you explain, Gorget," asked Tom, "exactly where we're going tomorrow? I don't understand yet your earlier comment about the Bastard King's castle being 'straight down.'"

"That's one thing I'm afraid I can't do," said Gorget honestly. "It's entirely beyond me to fully convey what you're going to see. You'll just have to wait till morning."

Since the sparse, monochromatic illumination of the scarlet land seemed as unvarying as its weather, having shown no changes in all the hours they had walked, Tom was unable to figure out how morning made itself known. He refrained from asking, however, fearing to confound Gorget further.

Nathan ventured a question, speaking for the first time since helping Tom up off the floor.

"Gorget, you referred to Glimmerglitch as your wife. May I ask by what rites and vows you have sanctified your union?"

Scratching his bald pate, Gorget took a moment to interpret Nathan's phrasing. "I don't rightly know as we ever employed any such things, Master Shiverick. When we were ready to mate, we did, and we've been together ever since, through six litters." After a brief pause, Gorget added, "We do usually have a special meal to celebrate the day we built our house, if that's anything like what you mean."

Nathan was about to clarify what he meant — possibly with many divagations relating to original sin, predestined grace and holy sacraments — when Natty cut in.

"Nahum, you greedy soul-snatcher, leave these fine folks alone. Can't you see that they're far advanced above your petty creed? Conventions have no hold on them, anymore than they do on Tom and myself." Natty turned to Tom and gripped his arm, as if to drive home his point. "Remember our first conversation, Tom, in the rhododendron grove, when you confided in me about seeking a life beyond conventions? Well, *voila*, here you have it! Observe this prosperous couple, beholden to no one, living a life of simple pleasures, unfettered by cumbersome ethics. Surely their Liege must lead an even more gracious existence. When we arrive tomorrow, let us all apply for permanent residence in his court. Forget Mab, Tom. Your quest ends here!"

Natty released Tom and took in the hut and what lay beyond with an expansive sweep of his arm.

Tom stared at Natty with total disbelief. Had the dapper fellow gone completely crazy? What did he see in this grim place that so attracted him? Perhaps the privations they had jointly undergone were affecting him more cruelly than they were Tom and Nathan, who cared less for their own comfort.

"No sense rushing into anything, Natty," Tom cautioned, trying to humor his friend. "Let's get to the King's court first, before we make up our minds."

Natty stood irritably. "*Bah*! I had thought you a less timid fellow than most, but you're just as bad. I'll plead my own case, at least, tomorrow. You do what you want."

Stalking to a corner and throwing himself down, Natty offered them his hostile back.

The outburst having put an end to conversation, the others retired also.

Tom found it hard to fall asleep. He was jittery with anticipation of the morrow. In addition, the red glare of the smoldering sky filtered through the roof and seemed to scorch his eyes right through his lowered lids.

Turning over onto his stomach, he caught a glimpse of the trolls disrobing. The sight of Gorget's oversized genitals took him aback. He hid his face against the wall. However, this did not shut out the sound of the trolls' enthusiastic coupling. Later, he finally sank into an uneasy slumber.

"Morning" broke: a time only marginally different from any other. Tom awoke as if from a fever, confused and uncertain of his whereabouts. Like notes in a hundred bottles, everything washed up on memory's strand after a moment, and he rose with aching muscles, eager to reach the first monarch he must pay homage to, before he could meet Mab's obscure criteria for learning more about Faerie.

Initially, he was unable to return Gorget's and Glimmerglitch's frank good-morning greetings without embarrassment, after their performance last night. But soon he reconciled his sensibilities to their different attitudes towards privacy, reminding himself that, after all, it was their house.

A dipper of scummy water apiece and some johnnycakes that were burnt on the outside and wet within constituted their breakfast. Then, bidding children and wife farewell, Gorget ushered the four travellers out into the street.

Leaving his beetle hitched, Gorget led the way on foot.

Yesterday, upon their arrival in the rambling town, the streets had been empty, all the citizens presumably in their tumbledown cottages. But as they made their way behind their guide today, the three men and the fachan found themselves joining a veritable river of bodies, all heading in the same direction, as if they were droplets in a common flood, rushing toward a precipice.

Through the narrow, twisty streets the crowd of trolls surged, male and female alike, all with the same unguessable destination. Tom had to strive to keep his little band together, and within sight of Gorget.

At last, Gorget hustled them into a relatively empty sidestreet, where they could catch their breath. "We'll wait until the majority of the workers descend," he said. "Then we'll go down. No sense taking a chance that you'll get pushed over the side by the crush."

No one felt inclined to ask for amplification of his remarks.

When the flood had subsided to a trickle, Gorget led

them out of the sanctuary, saying, "Just a bit further. Keep your spirits up."

Gorget had not lied about the distance. After covering only a hundred yards, they exited from between two typical houses and stopped dead in their tracks, confronted with a spectacle that chilled their blood.

They stood on the rim of a vast pit or quarry, fully a mile across. Houses were built nearly up to the edge all around, behind the backs of the foursome and circling away to the far side. The more distant structures looked like anthills, a few trolls among them like mites. The pit seemed to be filled with the ugly light of the red sky, so that it resembled a pustulent sore. From where they stood, Tom could not see the bottom.

"Lucky for you," said Gorget, "that I happen to live near the head of the ramp. Otherwise, we might have had to skirt the whole construction to the other side."

Gorget's words caused Tom to notice that a few trolls still hurried past them, and seemed to toss themselves over the edge. Tom realized that, contrary to appearances, they must have been using the ramp Gorget mentioned.

"We're to go down into this hole?" Tom asked, already knowing the answer.

"Why, of course. It's where the palace is. Come along, now. We must hurry to reach the King by noon. I'll answer any questions you have as we descend."

Gorget led them right up to the precipice. They looked in. Chaos looked back.

A ramp threaded the inner sides of the funnel-shaped pit. It wound counterclockwise, a gyre to the underworld. This widdershins ramp began immediately at their feet. The spiral was crowded with confusing activity unintelligible at this distance. Faint noises — as of hammering, cursing, banging, squealing, shouting, screaming and thudding — drifted up from the pit. Tom almost wished a god-sized screw would be driven from the heavens above into this pit to prevent them from entering.

Tom's vision naturally followed the path of the spiral underfoot: down and around, down and around, down and around —

Dizzy, he reached its end. The bottom of the pit seemed the size of a florin. It had to be half a mile straight down.

Lug hopped back nervously from the edge, shaking his head. Nathan crossed himself. Even Natty seemed to lose a bit of his nonchalance. Although sick at heart, Tom faced them all squarely and said, "There's no turning back now, men — and fachan. Let's go."

Reluctantly they embarked upon the descent.

The ramp was wide enough for six to walk comfortably abreast.

They went single file, hugging the wall on their right.

Gorget began to deliver an impromptu lecture over his shoulder as they moved slowly down the gradual slope. It served to keep Tom's mind off the alarming drop directly to his left, with certain death waiting at the end. He hoped the others were deriving similar benefit from the troll's chatter.

"Our pit," Gorget began proudly, "is over five centuries old. Each day during that period, we workers have descended this ramp to the floor of the pit, where we labor to excavate deeper and deeper. Actually, of course, there are two shifts at the pit, a day and night crew. So while one group is going down, the other is coming up the ramp. At the top, the offshift gang follows a different road through the town than the crew going on duty. Traffic monitors spaced regularly coordinate the flow."

"What — what are you digging for?" Tom asked between nervous glances to his left.

"Oh, my badness!" Gorget said. "I thought you knew. Why, Hell, of course."

Tom found no voice to question further, but Gorget gleefully went on with the story.

"Before there was a pit at all, there was the court of the Bastard King, capitol of the Scarlet Empire." (Again, that disturbing name that Tom felt he should remember from somewhere. But the oppressive heat and strange circumstances kept his mind from functioning as it should.) "The court was known far and wide as the most evil spot on this mortal earth. They revelled in their reputation, as they do today, and did everything they could to uphold it. One day, however, a silver-haired witch wandered into the kingdom. She was taken before the King, who tried to subdue her to his will, but failed. This witch, after bursting the bonds placed upon her, laughed and said, 'King, thou art but a pale imitation of Hell, and since even that court holds no dominion over me, you most certainly do not.' Then she vanished.

"Well, the King could not take any revenge on this woman, but he determined instantly to find out if what she had said was true. He ordered the digging toward Hell to commence. And what is more, he decided he would bring his palace down with him."

Before Gorget could go on to reveal the method the King had chosen to bring his castle with him, the party was stopped in their tracks by a troll wearing a brassard of red cloth around one knotty bicep. This, Tom thought, had to be one of the traffic monitors. With upraised hand, the monitor barred their way, refusing to let them pass, and indicating that they should press themselves as closely as possible against the wall.

Soon the reason why became evident.

First a rumbling sounded from lower down on the slope. It grew louder and louder, until the source of it came into view.

A giant beetle bigger than a horse walked backwards on its forelegs, rolling an enormous boulder in the same manner in which a dung-scarab propels its ball. Behind it came several trolls, bearing buckets full of dirt and rubble on yokes across their backs.

When the excavators had passed, the monitor signalled that Gorget's group could continue. This was accomplished by a titanic blow delivered upside Gorget's head.

Tom started, expecting a fight. But Gorget merely cringed, saying, "Thank you, sir. Much too kind of you. We'll be on our way now."

They went past the monitor, who ignored the humans.

When they had gone a little distance, Gorget, one pointy ear swelling, turned to Tom and smiled sheepishly. "He outranked me," said the troll, by way of explanation for his superior's behavior.

Tom felt sad on behalf of the mannikin, who had been so friendly to them, but said nothing, thinking any commiseration would just make Gorget's lot more miserable.

The incident with the monitor had evidently driven any further thoughts of lecturing from Gorget's mind, and the rest of the trip was made in silence, save for the jumble of sounds arising from the pit.

Around and around the spiral wound, seemingly interminable. Many more times they were halted by traffic-trolls, so that upward-struggling laborers could pass. Work-beetles in abundance pushed their loads up the ramp. The noise from below became steadily louder, until it reached ear-troubling proportions.

All the workers seemed to function willingly, without close supervision, as if they had long been indoctrinated to their proper tasks. Still, an occasional overseer was encountered. These were burly bare-chested humans wearing leather skirts fashioned of two flapping panels, and carrying long whips with weighted tails. Without provocation they would lash out at the grunting, sweating trolls, laying open backs and faces, buttocks and calves.

The first time Tom saw such treatment, he almost leapt upon the overseer, who had laid low a faltering female troll. Only Lug hopping into his path held Tom back until he regained his commonsense. His interference would only get him — and possibly the others — killed. It would be little comfort if the overseer were later punished. Tom continued the descent, looking away each time he came upon such a scene. Still, his blood boiled.

Eventually the fatiguing and circuitous journey came to an end. The five individuals stepped out onto a level plain, whose very flatness seemed an aberration, after the constant slope. Tom and the rest looked about in amazement.

The bottom diameter of the pit was not a mile, due to the slanting sides. Still many acres spread away before them. Activity was everywhere. Trolls with shovels attacked the sides of the pit and the bottom. Buckets were filled and hoisted onto shoulders. Rocks were pounded and cracked. Whips snapped through the air. Across the pit, Tom noticed something he at first refused to admit was possible.

A scorpion big as a barn dug its claws into the wall, crumbling strata easily. A troll sat atop it, guiding it. Its barbed tail was held arching over its back.

Gorget noticed Tom's stare. "Wonderful beasts," he

said. "They actually do double duty, for when they get old and worn-out, we use them for food. That was the meat in your toadstools last night."

Tom's stomach turned over. A queasy look passed across Nathan's face, and Natty blanched.

Directing their attention to a portion of the pit as yet unsurveyed by the newcomers, Gorget said proudly: "Gentlemen, the castle of the Bastard King!"

This was what Tom saw.

A distant pillar of stone rose up fifty feet from the current lowermost level of the pit, like a mesa with a broad flat top about an acre in extent. Obviously, the top of the mesa had once been the bottom of the pit. A rock ramp that was integral with the mesa led up to the top.

The castle sat atop the mesa. From Tom's vantage, because of the airborne quarry dust and pervading gloom, he could see only one huge wooden wheel supporting a crouching immensity.

"When the pillar is a hundred feet tall," Gorget explained, "having been undercut on all sides, the ramp leading down will then extend almost all the way across the floor to one pit wall. Then, controlling its speed with ropes, we'll roll the castle down to its new level, and demolish the old pillar. Afterwards, the whole process starts again, the castle travelling back and forth across the pit."

Tom shook his head at the enormous effort that went into this folly.

Gorget clapped his hands with satisfaction, contemplating the joyous day.

"Let's get a move on," he said. "The King's expecting you."

6

The Bastard King

"Fair is foul, and foul is fair . . ."
— William Shakespeare, *Macbeth*

When he saw the sentries standing at their posts like eidolons, Tom realized at last — with a sickening sensation of fear and anger, sorrow and rage — exactly whose web he was entering.

But by then he was almost too tired to care.

When Gorget had deemed that his little tour-group had had long enough to appreciate the spectacle laid out before them, he had moved briskly off toward the foot of the ramp leading to the top of the butte.

Tom and the others wearily picked up their feet and followed. Across the gritty, treacherous cinders and clinkers they made their halting way, the cacophony of the pit battering at their ears.

Alone among them, Natty seemed insusceptible to fatigue. He bounced merrily along, as if growing stronger and stronger, the closer he got the throne of the Bastard King.

As he walked, Tom tried, in a hazy fashion, to figure out how long their descent had been. If the pit were a mile across, then its circumference was roughly three miles. If the spiral dropped, say, one hundred feet with every revolution, and the bottom of the pit was half a mile down, then there were what — twenty-five complete turns of the gyre, times three. . . .

It kept coming up seventy-five miles, no matter how Tom figured it. But that was sheerly impossible. They could never have covered that distance, without rest or food. And how could the trolls do it every day? No, he had to have misplaced a decimal point somewhere.

Yet come to think of it, how far had they really walked upon the Great Road, once beneath the burgundy sky? Tom found he retained no clear idea of distances or time in this scarlet land. It seemed as if he had been walking forever, was uncounted leagues away from the fork where he had left Mab, yet still somehow as close to her as when they had sat side by side in the flowered lea. Had his brief contact with Mab already endowed him with something of the legendary Faerie power to transcend space? Were his perceptions of *near* and *far* altering, till that familiar and seemingly irreconcilable dichotomy was replaced by an unthinkable synchronicity?

Tom had no easy answer. He only knew that no snapping of his fingers would bring him to the castle hulking like a vulture atop the butte. That would be accomplished only by placing one leaden foot ahead of the other, time after time.

So he did it.

When they reached the base of the stone ramp that was of a piece with the mesa, Tom experienced a brief irony that they should have to ascend, after going down for so long. Gorget led them past the busy workers at the foot of the ramp, and they labored upward, new leg muscles coming into play and bearing the brunt of the climb.

Lungs straining to take in the dirty dark air, they toiled upward.

At last they set foot upon the tabletop.

Tom's revelation as to the true identity of his host was waiting.

But the first thing he noticed was the true shape of the castle, which had been concealed till now by murk and distance and Tom's inattention.

The building was an effigy on wheels. Its shape was that of a long-snouted, couchant lizard, whose extended forepaws gripped an enormous axle. The wooden lizard had its mouth agape, its lower toothed jaw forming a sloping entrance into the building. Chains depending from the upper jaw — roughly where one would normally find the canine teeth — seemed to indicate that the ramp could be drawn up, closing the door at will.

The scale of the structure was titanic. The wheels were twice as tall as a man. The windows that signified the eyes of the lizard were perhaps five stories above the ground.

The whole structure was red. Tom suddenly realized that to say it was painted would have been incorrect. Stained was a better word. Its sides were besmeared with layers of clotted grue, round which swarmed innumerable flies. It was as if catapults had bombarded the building with countless sanguineous corpses. A stench of decay rose from it, an offense to the mind as well as the nose.

Standing by the upright wooden teeth in the lower jaw were two sentries. Tom finally focused on them.

Recognition screamed like a banshee in his brain.

The sentries wore laquered red armor. The butts of their fleur-de-lys lances were grounded in the grit underfoot. Longswords hung at their hips. Lowered visors kept them faceless.

These were the invaders who had burst into Tom's life and propelled him willy-nilly on this very journey. Their leader must wait inside. The Bastard King — this had been the name the second invading party had used on that horrible night some months ago for the man they chased.

Tom's mind swam in a sea of turbulent emotions. Should he give way to his anger, or cower in abject fear? Thoughts of fleeing, and others of taking vengeance, battled for control of his limbs. Spasms shook him, as he recalled his mother's bone-rattling coughs. He felt he might go mad.

Three hands upon him brought him back to reality. Two were Nathan's, one Lug's. His friends gazed with concern upon him. Not knowing this portion of his history, they were baffled as to the cause of his sudden fit.

"I'm — I'm all right," Tom said.

A wave of inexplicable calmness washed over him as he spoke these words. He felt emptied of all hostility and trepidation, as if viewing a distant passion-play that had no bearing on his life. This feeling lasted only seconds, passing in turn to be followed by a more normal interest in his own affairs. He knew with certainty that anything that happened now — however important and pregnant with consequences for his future the events to come might be — would occur without reference to the past. The process of disengaging himself from the preterite burden all men dragged behind them like heavy fardels — the process begun with his kirkyard epiphany — had just been carried another long step forward.

Nathan and Lug released Tom reluctantly, as if still believing he might collapse. Tom tried to reassure them and also communicate something of his newfound intuitions.

"What are we waiting for, friends?" Tom said bravely. "Let's greet the rascals inside this Trojan Newt, before it vomits them out!"

Natty came from behind to slap Tom's shoulder in a hail-fellow-well-met fashion. "That's the kind of talk we need, Tom! Why do we tarry? Let us hasten forward to meet these single-minded burrowers as equals, and demand our share of their bounty."

Before Tom could reply that this was not what he meant, Natty had bounded ahead, setting foot on the jaw of the castle. The sentries made no move to block him, evidently having orders to let them pass.

Tom motioned for the others to follow, and they proceeded behind Natty.

As Nathan stepped beneath the upper jaw, he muttered something about "into the belly of the beast." But he followed, however reluctantly.

The interior of the castle was painted in a more conventional fashion, everywhere a dull madder. Tom felt as if he were actually being swallowed by a living creature, sucked inward to be chewed by rear molars and digested.

The ramp debouched into what would have been the lizard's palate. Two more sentries kept watch here. These carried pennants Tom remembered only too well: a lizard rampant with extended tongue. The level floor of the mouth stretched away to right and left. A couple of smoky torches dimly illuminated the huge cavern of the mouth, whose ceiling hung half-seen far overhead. Above must be the hollow cranium, with its eye-windows.

At the back of the mouth, a wide staircase ascended the arched gullet. Pairs of sentries stood on each stair, so motionless that Tom thought them carved.

"I'll lead from here," Gorget said, moving out in front of Tom, Nathan and Lug, who clustered closely for comfort. Natty acquiesced with a sardonic bow. The rock-solid troll seemed both nervous and excited, as if simultaneously dreading and anticipating what was to come. "I've only been here once before," he confided, "but I remember the way."

With this, he led them to the stairs. Up they went, at last reaching the apex of the throat.

For some reason, Tom had expected that the interior of the lizard would be entirely hollow. He thought they would confront a vast, echoing space like an empty barrel. How they would descend to the floor of the belly, he had no idea. A long slide, another staircase, a ladder? He was prepared for any of these. Instead, he encountered nothing but a rather conventional anteroom, as broad as the beast's shoulders, with a high arched ceiling conforming to the lizard's back. Tapestries depicting warfare hung on the walls.

Tom suddenly realized that the structure, far from being like a barrel, was rather like a ship: many interconnected decks. The prosaic nature of the interior gave him something to hang onto.

Upon their arrival, one of the inevitable brace of sentries had disappeared through huge double doors set in the far wall. Gorget kept his charges waiting now for the soldier's return.

A few minutes later, the doors were thrown open.

Trumpets blared beyond the doors, announcing the arrival of outsiders.

Gorget hustled them through the entrance.

Tom found himself in a room that ran the remaining length of the lizard-castle. Several hundred yards long, and wide as the beast, it was bisected by a red carpet that unrolled like an extension of the Great Road straight back toward what appeared — at this distance — to be a dais supporting two thrones. Against each wall stood a serried rank of armored warriors at attention. There must have been close to a thousand, thought Tom. Above their plumed casques, torches at intervals cast a light like that of a sun gone feeble with age. Interspersed with the torches were the mounted skulls of various animals. Horned and grinning, nostrils gaping, the skulls had been imperfectly cured. Tatters of hide and desiccated flesh and sinew hung from them, scenting the air with a charnel odor. It was as if the heads had been brought back from the hunt, dripping blood, and immediately nailed to the wall, there to putrefy. Above the skulls, rafters hoarded shadows. Straining his eyes, Tom seemed to discern a curve to the ceiling, as it arched to form the lizard's shape.

Gorget whispered, "Do just as I say," and began to tread the red carpet toward the dais. Perforce, his charges followed.

As they walked, Tom found a headache blooming between his eyes, directly behind the bridge of his nose. It dawned on him that the source of his uncommon neuralgia was all this red. He had never realized how deadly stifling a single color, repeated *ad infinitum*, could be. He longed for a little green or silver to break the monotony. But only a hundred shades of that crimson sliver of the spectrum answered his beseeching gaze.

The awesome, silent rows of knights recalled to Tom how they had ridden into the clearing around his home on that night when his life had been turned upside down. He could picture them swarming out of the giant wooden lizard like maggots from a corpse, marching to the stables where their big chestnut horses were tossing their manes, mounting the beasts and riding clanking off across the floor of the pit. At the foot of the upward gyre they would draw up two abreast and begin the ascent. Round and round they would spiral, in a dizzy race to the top. Laborers would be brushed off the spiral if they did not move aside fast enough, falling to their doom. When the riders reached the top, they would stampede through troll-town, smashing huts and bodies. Once upon the scarlet branch of the Great Road, they would ride —

Where? Tom's re-creation of that night broke down at this point. He knew that the horde had not come through Ercildoune and the surrounding countryside. No one had ever heard of them in those parts. And their tracks, which he and Uncle Ross had investigated, with many a puzzled head-scratching — those tracks began in mid-gallop, and disappeared the same way.

How had the outriders of the Scarlet Empire come to the Rhymer croft? And why?

Tom gave up the riddle, seeking to concentrate all his wits upon the imminent meeting with the Bastard King.

The closer they got to the throne-platform, Tom noticed, the worse the stink of decay. A look to the mounted trophies revealed why. Those near the door had been the oldest, and hence picked the cleanest by insects and time. The heads grew more recent as one marched up the room, until now they were still festering, rotting, meat-covered things, nailed crudely against the wall. Insects feasted on them with a muted buzzing.

At this end of the room, big trestle tables and accompanying benches flanked the carpet, as if the court dined here. Although bare at this moment, the tables reminded Tom of how hungry and thirsty he was. The travellers had not eaten since the breakfast in Gorget's house, and, if they had indeed walked anything like the distance Tom had calculated, it was a wonder they could even stand now. He wondered if their host's hospitality would extend to a meal, or if the constraints Mab had placed on him merely covered granting them an audience.

Soon he would learn, for they were almost at the platform.

When Gorget abruptly stopped, some distance from the dais, and hurled himself face-first to the floor, Tom was taken aback. Were they supposed to imitate this grovelling? He'd be damned if he would! Tom remained erect, gesturing to his companions to do likewise.

Gorget looked up from his prostrate position. Terror was written plain on his babyish features.

"Get down, get down!" he hissed. "You don't know what you're doing!"

"I won't," Tom loudly replied. He stepped over Gorget and advanced closer to the thrones. At the edge of the dais he halted, and took in the scene.

The broad platform bore two royal seats. The most imposing held the Bastard King.

Here was the giant who had commanded the burning of Tom's cottage. Unarmored now, he wore red, fur-trimmed robes encrusted with rubies. Across his lap he held a colossal sword. His face was as Tom had once seen it: a twisted topography of pulsing veins and massive bones, twitching muscles and cavernous eye-sockets. What had been concealed by his armor, however, was the fact that he was bald. The round dome of his head, whether shaven or naturally clean, was absolutely hairless. Its prominences and clefts were a text any phrenologist would have shuddered to read.

Occupying the throne beside the King was a woman.

Next to Mab, she was the most beautiful creature Tom had ever seen.

Her russet tresses reminded Tom of autumnal foliage. Torchlight caught in her eyes, imparting a fulgent carnelian cast to them. Her lips were painted cherry-red. She wore only diaphanous vermilion silks, which clung to her heavy breasts and thighs in a revealing fashion. Tom found it hard to tear his gaze away from her form.

Surrounding the royal couple was an assortment of courtiers. The men were slim and dangerous as rapiers, the women lush and alluring as satin pillows. Many of the courtiers reclined in pairs, the men idly squeezing their concubines.

Tom couldn't fathom, for a moment, the construction of the couches and chairs they used. Then his eyes accepted the truth.

Cushioned litters rested on the backs of kneeling trolls. Other trolls functioned as footstools. Their faces were carefully noncommittal, although sweat beaded their grooved brows.

Lying about like serpents among the courtiers were starved and vicious-looking roan whippets, their thin flanks shivering as if in anticipation of a chase.

Just as Tom finished his survey, the Bastard King's voice boomed out.

"Those who approach me must cast themselves into the dirt!"

To his amazement, Tom found that the King's formidable appearance and tone had little effect on him. The fact that he had seen this man before, from his hiding place in the woods, and knew him for what he was, while at the same time the King had no idea of who Tom might be — this fact filled Tom with a curious satisfaction and strength, as if he somehow had the upper hand on the man.

Not knowing where his words came from, Tom spoke.

"She who sent me said nothing of paying such tribute. I will bow to you and your lady" — here Tom gave
two curt nods — "as any visitor might. But I will not cast
myself at your feet."

Hearing Tom, all the courtiers stopped their idle
dalliance. Seemingly thrilled, the titian-haired woman
strained forward in her chair toward Tom, her eager
breathing agitating her bosom, like a hawk about to fall
upon prey. Everyone waited for the King's reaction to
Tom's affrontery.

The scarlet Liege's hand gripped the pommel of his
sword so tightly that his knuckles stood out white. Mention of Mab seemed to have offended him more than
Tom's refusal to fall down. A deep rumbling started low
in his chest, swelling by degrees until it became a full-
throated roar. Still seated, he swept his sword up above
his head, as if to cleave Tom from skull to crotch.

Tom stood without trembling, knowing with some
sourceless yet infallible certainty that his end was not
here, not yet.

With an enormous bellow, the King hurled his sword
as if it were a mere dirk. But its course was toward one
wall, and it passed by Tom harmlessly. End over end it
spun, light as a feather, deadly as an adder.

After crossing the wide room, the weapon still had
force enough upon one downswing to penetrate the
armor of an unflinching warrior, piercing him and pin-
ning him with two feet of emergent blade to the wall like
a bright butterfly.

A timorous round of gentle applause sounded from the courtiers. The King's Consort sank back into her throne, a satisfied smile twisting her cherry lips, her form lax as if sated from orgasm.

Tom was appalled. He bit his tongue, knowing that he could only step so far out of bounds. Wondering what to do next, he decided to try to placate the King with a gift. He still hoped, after all, to wrangle a meal from him! Having so few possessions, though, Tom was at a loss what to offer. Finally, he hit upon his book. From his wallet he took the volume that had once meant the world to him.

"Sire," Tom said, "I offer you this splendid tract, which speaks at length of the Hell you seek, as a small recompense for your audience."

Placing one foot on the dais, Tom gingerly extended the book. The King, after a moment of puzzlement, snatched it. Holding it upside down, he riffled through the pages. Then, with an effortless twitch, he ripped the leather-clad book in half.

Tom sucked in a sharp breath. Half the book was tossed back at his feet. The other half the King threw at one of his courtiers, catching the man in the stomach.

The King addressed his man, who had risen from a chaise and stood now with a look of fear on his features.

"Eat it!" said the King.

Without a moment's hesitation, the courtier raised the book to his lips and bit off a mouthful of paper, which he began earnestly to chew.

Tom picked up the other half of his book. It was the rear half. The new first page, Tom saw, was the first page of Paradise. Purgatory and Hell had become the courtier's meal. Not knowing what to think, Tom tucked the raped book back in his scrip.

The Bastard King gazed at his Consort. She gave an almost imperceptible nod of her head, and licked her lips.

"Queen Lilith," said the King, "reminds me of our duty to guests. I proclaim a feast! After these strangers have refreshed themselves, and the proper preparations have been made, the revellry will commence! Also, we must reward our faithful servant, who brought them here.

"Gorget!" shouted the King. "Stand up!"

The troll rose, quivering.

"Guards, take Gorget to the kitchens, and make him a meal."

The King clapped his hands and two sentries detached themselves from the wall. The gutted man was not one of them. Tom wondered if he would stay there like the animal heads, till only a skeleton in armor remained.

The troll bowed a dozen times before the guards reached him. "Thank you, Your Illegitimacy, thank you. You honor me too greatly. Most obliged. Thank you . . ."

Tom watched wistfully as the mannikin was shepherded from the room, his profuse thanks growing fainter with each step. He wondered if he and Gorget would ever meet again.

Two more warriors had taken up positions behind the visitors.

"Show these four to their rooms," the King commanded.

At the news that they were to be separated, Tom grew nervous. Kept apart, how would he and the others use Lug to return to Mab, if an emergency presented itself?

"King," Tom began, "could we not all have but a single room —"

Crack! The King held in one ogreish hand the left arm of his throne, a carved wood piece thick as Tom's bicep, which the King had just effortlessly snapped off. Veins throbbed in the King's forehead, and Tom could hear the giant's teeth grinding.

Nathan was at Tom's side, whispering. "Ask the fachan if the spell will still work upon us all, no matter the distance separating us."

Tom bent low to Lug. "Lug — how far apart can we all be, and still be rescued by my calling on Mab?"

Lug held up five fingers.

"Oh, great," Tom said, remembering Lug's lack of facility with higher math. He rephrased the question. "Can we get so far apart in this castle that you and I won't be able to include Natty and Nathan in our protection?"

Lug violently shook his head no.

Tom straightened, hoping Lug had understood him aright. "Very well, Sire, we accept whatever rooms you assign us. Providing this fachan remains with me."

The King seemed to have tired of these petty annoyances. He waved his hands in dismissal, and leaned away from Tom to confer in a low rumble with Queen Lilith.

Tom turned from the dais toward his companions.

Natty's appearance dumbfounded him.

The foxy fellow, despite his vows to state his case, had remained silent throughout the interview. Tom now saw the reason why.

Natty stood on tiptoe, as if some puppeteer yanked his strings. He was straining toward Queen Lilith, as if he and she were two lodestones of opposite polarity, and longed to fuse. The Consort, for her part, ignored the man, apparently absorbed in speech with the King, save for an occasional glance at Tom.

Feeling as if he were watching unknown elemental forces at work, Tom feared to interrupt. But there was no choice. He moved to touch Natty, who responded as if sleepwalking.

As a group, the four departed the great hall.

Tom was sure they would retrace their steps — as Gorget had done — until they returned to the vicinity of the lizard's neck. However, this was not to be.

The guards led the four at an angle across the vast room. Close to one wall, they stopped at a spot seemingly devoid of significance. One of the silent guards bent and gripped an iron ring nearly invisible in the gloom. Heaving, he lifted a trapdoor. A set of stairs led down.

Beckoned brusquely to descend, Tom and his friends complied.

The stairs ended in the middle of a corridor — wide by the standards Tom employed, but nowhere near the dimensions of the single immense room above. Obviously this new level was divided into smaller rooms and halls. The ceiling, some twelve feet high, was flat, and had Tom not known differently, he might have believed they were in a conventionally built castle, instead of the actual architectural conceit which had swallowed them.

One guard in the lead, the other following, the party — after many turns and twists that left the visitors thoroughly confused — found themselves at three doors, set not too far apart in the same wall. The first door was opened, and Natty was motioned in. The second room gaped for Nathan. Tom and Lug soon found themselves ensconced in the third suite.

Tom's first impulse was to try the handle of his door, which, to his surprise, he found unlocked. Giving the matter further consideration, he realized that a lock would have been superfluous. Out of the room, where could he find safety in the castle? Out of the castle, who would shelter him in the whole Scarlet Empire?

With such thoughts to discomfit him, Tom turned his attention to the room.

A canopy-bed bulked like a pavilion in one corner of the large room. A waist-high chest of drawers across from the bed held an ewer of water, which Tom fell upon like a man desert-bound for weeks. When he had slaked his thirst, he guiltily remembered Lug, who stood patiently nearby, flexing his knee in anticipation of a drink. Tom passed the pitcher to him.

While the fachan drank, Tom studied his own reflection in a mirror he noticed above the chest. The smoky glass held in its depths a figure he doubted he would have recognized, had he met him face to face.

Tom's cheeks were sunken, and his stubble — - although never thick — was more pronounced than when he had last seen himself, in Mab's spring. Her pale seal still graced his jaw. The perpetual doubtful quirk which had clung to his mouth since adolescence had become almost derisory. His oafish smock and trews hung improbably on him, scarecrow-fashion. What sort of adventurer did he resemble? Perhaps one of those sainted Irish maniacs, who were always setting out to sea in a stone trough and ending up on islands populated by savages eager for conversion.

Tom turned away from his reflection, looking for Lug, whom he hoped to question about this strange court they found themselves in. How Lug would have conveyed any information, Tom did not know. Perhaps he could learn to read the fachan's face as well as Mab did. And thinking of Mab made Tom wonder why she hadn't told him more about this land. She knew his whole story, and must surely have been aware that the Bastard King was the one who had terrorized him and his mother so long ago. But then, he was on a mission to learn things. And didn't learning consist of finding things out for one's self?

In any case, Lug was not disposed to answer a single question. He lay sleeping like a log upon the bed, his single arm sticking straight up from his chest. His wide nostrils gently quivered as he breathed long and calmly.

Tom stepped softly toward a three-legged chair he had spotted, intending to follow Lug's example.

A knock sounded at the door.

Who the hell —? thought Tom.

He went to the door and cautiously opened it.

Queen Lilith awaited without.

But not for long.

Pushing the door inward, the Consort insinuated herself without invitation, and shut the door behind herself.

Her musky scent, like a civet cat's and so dissimilar to Mab's floral perfume, filled the air around Tom. His headache did not vanish, but rather underwent a strange transformation, becoming a tumescent demon in his skull.

Lilith stood so closely to Tom that he could see every tiniest crease in her painted lips. It seemed that only the thickness of her sheer silks separated his body from hers.

"The King," said Lilith, in a voice like butter coated with poisoned honey, "has bid me escort you on a tour of our palace."

Mention of the King shook Tom somewhat from his

stupor. "Well, that's very nice of you and, uh, His Illegiti-macy. But I don't know, I'm quite tired —"

"No, you're not," Lilith said.

And when she touched his hand with one red nail, it was true.

"Come," said Lilith, moving toward the door.

Tom looked toward the sleeping fachan, whom their *sotto voce* dialogue had not awakened. Lug had said they were safe apart. Did that mean out of earshot? What did he care about returning to Mab, anyway? He was on a mission to learn what he could . . .

"All right," Tom said dreamily. "But not for too long. We don't want to miss the feast."

Lilith smiled, her lips parting like a wound.

"We won't miss a thing," she promised.

Tom could not believe the sights Lilith had shown him. But that was all right. He was only dreaming them, it seemed. One was not bound to believe that which occurred in dreams. Pay attention to such visions, perhaps, as harbingers or warnings. But most definite-ly not believe in their reality. Because if one did — well, some of the creations of Morpheus could be quite nasty.

Had he really seen, for instance, dungeons and tor-ture cells in the belly of the beast, replete with wailing, agony-racked trolls? Or the cushioned room whose floor he first thought was a pulsating organism — until he recognized it for a sea of writhing, naked humans, coupling with each other and with various scaly beasts? Certainly he had only dreamed that beneath the tail of the lizard there had been a mock-sphincter, with a catapult positioned before it, from which hogtied (but not gagged, for how could one then enjoy their screams?) trolls were shot out across the pit.

No, these and other, more disturbing visions were only the byproducts of a tired body and confused mind. They had to be. Why, he was probably stretched out beside Lug on the bed right now, tossing uneasily in the grip of his nightmares.

But yet, every time Lilith laid a soft hand on his arm, or came so close that her perfume filled his lungs as water flooded those of a drowning man, Tom had a disturbing intuition that he was not asleep, but that he was really walking through this castle of alien desires and compulsions, at his side an unknown woman whose interest in him was rather alarming.

Now they stood at the foot of a iron spiral staircase that corkscrewed up through the ceiling, and thence — Tom couldn't say. Had they just descended it, or were they about to begin the climb?

"Have you seen all you wish to see, Thomas?" Lilith asked sweetly.

Tom couldn't remember ever mentioning his name to Lilith. But Gorget had hailed them by name upon the Great Road. That's right, they had been expected. But who was it who had sent word ahead of them? Vague images of a silver-haired witch came to Tom. What was her name?

Shaking off the confusing memories, Tom said, "I suppose so. But there was something else — What was it?" His mind wasn't working right in this dream. He gazed into Lilith's sparkling red eyes, as if that would help him think. Red eyes — That was it. From outside the lizard-castle, he had seen ruby windows in its skull that mimicked eyes.

"We haven't been inside the head yet," Tom said. "Let's go there."

Lilith's tongue teased her lips apart, as if tasting the cherry-paint thereon, before retreating into the moist cavern of her mouth. "Why, Thomas, those are my private rooms in the skull of our castle. Surely you don't mean to invite yourself there?"

Tom's mind seemed to have been suddenly possessed by the fixation that he should visit the beast's head. "Yes," he petulantly said, "that's where I want to go. I don't care whose rooms are there."

Lilith fastened both hands on Tom's upper left arm. "Oh, Thomas, you're so direct that I couldn't refuse. Follow me, then, my rogue."

Lilith started up the spiral stairs, and Tom came behind.

Ahead and above Tom, Lilith's hips and buttocks wove a hypnotic pattern beneath their thin coverings. He couldn't tear his eyes away, looking neither left nor right nor down throughout the entire climb, following this eternal woman, always a few steps ahead of him, in an endless gyre that seemed to stretch along the dimension of time rather than space.

At last, though, the pursuit ended. Lilith and Tom emerged through a round trapdoor in the dorsal side of the castle. Tom looked around with befuddlement.

They stood outside on a narrow flat catwalk that ran along the curved spine of the lizard. Heat smote them like a mailed fist. Above, the somber red sky smoldered like a trashfire. It was at least seventy feet down to the mesa-top, another fifty to the pit-floor. From below, the crazy symphony of rocks being broken and backs being lashed floated up to them upon their precarious perch.

"This is the only way to reach my apartments," Lilith said. "Those who would visit me must show no fear."

"This doesn't bother me," Tom said, swaying drunkenly on the rail-less walk. "Let's go."

Smiling, Lilith led them toward the head.

As they walked, a question occurred to Tom.

"Lilith," he asked, "what will happen if the pit narrows too much to continue digging, before you reach Hell?"

Lilith halted and turned. The question had obviously infuriated her. "There is no chance we have miscalculated. And if we should, by some faint possibility, be in error — why then, we'll have our slaves widen the pit at the top and all the way down, if it takes a millennium!"

She resumed her sensuous walk, now with an overtone of anger, leaving Tom to advance or retreat, as he wished.

Tom followed.

At the neck — which sloped down toward the lowered head — the catwalk turned into a few dozen steps, running like a spinal crest to the wooden skull. Lilith trotted lightly down them. Tom moved more slowly, for here on the narrower neck, the drop-off was more alarming. Even in a dream, he did not care to fall such a distance.

At the lizard's occipitals, they came to a door, which Lilith pushed open.

In they went.

The room was suffused with a light the color of beets, and as thick as porridge, which poured in through the lizard's faceted eyes. Cushions were strewn casually about on a thick rug. A wardrobe and a dressing table, a chest and a garish oil-portrait of the Bastard King completed the furnishings.

Lilith sidled up to Tom. "I've been studying your face," she said. "It's so different from anyone else's I've ever seen. Especially those grey eyes. They remind me of someone who once visited us here, long ago, before even the pit was begun."

Pricking his cheek with a sharp nail, so as to draw a bead of blood, Lilith continued to regard Tom. "And this patch on your jaw. Wherever did you get so curious a scar?"

Tom strove to remember. But the effort was too great. Lilith seemed to take pity on his confusion, for she changed the subject.

"Come here to the window, and see the view."

They moved to the wall, and Lilith tossed open one massive casement. Peering out, Tom saw the top of the butte far below, and the pit stretching away beyond. He turned back to Lilith to compliment her on the vista.

Her silks were down around her waist. Rouged nipples made her breasts look like mounds of snow tinged by a sunset, atop which sat two scarabs.

"You can kiss these, Thomas," Lilith said, holding them for him. "But first I need a favor. Fetch me a feather I see there on the castle's snout."

"Out the window?" Tom said hazily.

"Yes. Just step out the window. You can scamper right down and back. And then we'll enjoy ourselves."

Tom placed a foot upon the window frame, and a hand on either side. He draw up his other foot, then stood erect in the tall window.

The snout was a slippery narrow ramp of boards, stretching away and down like the road to the heart of where nightmares were born. Tom didn't see any feather. But he'd give it a try.

He raised one foot and took a step —

The door into the skull burst open, its catch broken by the airborne form of Lug, who had obviously launched himself from midway down the spinal steps. The fachan hit the carpet, rolled and came to his foot. In a hop he was by the window, before Lilith could intervene. He grabbed Tom by his floppy shirt and hauled him back in.

Tom shook his head. The fachan's touch had awakened something in him. Where had he been going? What had gotten into him? He regarded the quizzical and distraught face of Lug, and bits and pieces of his past began to fall into place. Mab! How could he have forgotten her, and what she represented? He must have been out of his mind.

Lilith was fully clothed again, insofar as her original outfit merited that description. Her face was calm and unrevealing, neither guilty, gloating nor frustrated. Tom wondered if he had dreamed the whole crazy incident.

"You were worried about missing the feast," Lilith said neutrally. "I suspect it is about to begin. Let us return."

Without waiting for a response, Lilith hurried out.

Tom, feeling more and more like himself with each passing minute, looked about the room one last time, shuddering to think how close to death he had come. He laid a hand on Lug's feathery blue quills and said, "Thanks."

Lug bounced off the walls like a ball to signify, "Glad to help." Then they set out after the scarlet Consort.

Catching up with Lilith at the dorsal trapdoor, Lug and Tom were led by her back to their room. She bade them wait until called. Tom took advantage of the lull to rest.

After approximately half an hour, guards came for them. Out in the corridor, Tom and Lug were reunited with Nathan and Natty. Feeling a bit guilty for not having thought of his two friends in the recent confusion, Tom studied them to make sure they had not been abused or otherwise troubled while separated from him.

Nathan seemed the same gloomy specter as always, his undertaker's outfit, with its raggedly notched hat, looking positively homey amid all the gaudy redness.

Natty — Natty seemed to have undergone something exhausting. He did not exhibit the tetanic rigidity he had shown in the presence of Lilith, nor the absent-minded somnambulism of afterwards. Rather, he drooped and faltered, as if he had just carried the news to Marathon.

Tom came up to the drained dandy and laid a hand on his shoulder. "Are you okay, Natty?"

Jerking back as if rehearsing some awful incident, Natty said, "No, no more! I never knew —"

Tom shook his friend as if he were an apple tree reluctant to relinquish its fruit. "Snap out of it, Natty!"

Recognizing Tom at last, Natty said, "Oh, Tom lad, it's you. I thought — but it's nothing. Just anticipation of the festivities. Let's not keep our host and hostess" — here Natty quivered briefly — "waiting."

In the ruddy light of the corridor, Tom noticed a set of curious red marks on Natty's neck, as if the sucker-tipped arm of an octopus had enwrapped him. Tom gently touched one of the stigmata.

His finger came away tipped with cherry-paint.

"Natty —" Tom began.

But the man was already moving away down the hall.

Tom grinned ironically. Natty seemed unthankful that he had gotten what he had once so fervently desired.

The guards soon led them back to the huge hall where shadows cloistered among the beams and in the corners, and the decaying trophy heads diffused a noisome aroma. The nobles and the Bastard King and his Consort were already seated at the long tables.

Tom was escorted to the head of one table, to sit at the right hand of the King. A seat was open beside him, and two across the table, on the Consort's left. Lug moved to sit beside Tom, which would have left the Queen-side seats for Natty and Nathan. But at the last minute Natty pulled the chair next to Tom out from under Lug and took it for himself, as if eager to sit as far from Lilith as possible. Tom settled the dispute by giving in to Natty's choice, and Lug and Nathan sat side by side across the way.

The tables were draped with red cloths and set with crimson laquer-ware. Goblets stood at the head of each plate. No food was yet apparent.

The King stood. "Music!" he commanded.

The courtiers' heads swivelled unanimously in one direction, and Tom followed suit. A circular portion of the floor was descending. After a minute, it came back up, doubtlessly cranked by grunting trolls. On the circle was a gigantic pipe-organ, a troll seated at its keys. He began furiously to play, letting out all the stops and filling the hall with ominous moans and bellows that hurt the ears.

To this accompaniment the banquet began.

Down the length of the hall staggered four trolls bearing some sort of trough. As they got closer, Tom could see that it was the shell of one of the boulder-pushing beetles, filled with soup. While the servitors held the tureen, others ladled lumpy stew from it into individual, smaller shell bowls, which they set before the guests.

Tom tasted the soup tentatively, found it not overtly nauseating, and ate hungrily.

The waiters, meanwhile, moved from place to place, filling goblets from a glass pitcher. Lifting his spoon to his mouth, Tom accidentally jostled the troll pouring his drink. A drop or two splattered upon the cloth, sizzled and ate a hole there.

Tom stopped eating. The King, witnessing the accident, bade the troll fill his glass, which he then quaffed deeply.

"A liquor fit for men," the King said. "Equal parts scorpion poison and wormwood ale."

Nathan spoke up. "We have taken a vow of teetotalism for as long as we are on our quest, Sire."

"Yes, right, absolutely," Tom affirmed. "No spirits whatsoever."

The King scowled, then spat on the cloth. "Even our babes drink this, once they've been weaned. I count you pusillanimous milksops as less."

All the court members laughed uproariously, and drank deeply from their own glasses, as if to second the sentiment. Tom hung his head in anger and shame, wishing only to strike out at this Bastard King.

The second course arrived: big bloodless slabs of meat identified as scorpion steaks. Recalling that he had already tasted this delicacy at Gorget's house, Tom went ahead with the meal, thinking he might need every ounce of energy he could get.

After all the ravenous feasters had gorged themselves, the King raised his hand for silence. The booming notes of the organ stopped, as did all talk.

"The special treat!" bellowed the King.

Far down the hall, two trolls appeared bearing a platter. Tom turned his head for a moment as they neared, to observe the King and Lilith. On their faces were pasted twisted expressions more snarl than smile.

Tom heard the platter touch the table. He looked toward it.

Gorget kneeled naked upon the tray, his skin cracked and oozing juices, toadstool-stuffing spilling from his lips, his boiled eyes imploring Tom from beyond death.

" — make him a meal!" roared the King, as his sycophants cheered.

Tom shot to his feet and stalked off, trembling. No one stopped him, and, some feet from the table, he was joined by his companions. His brain was roiling like a cauldron. What could he do? Could he kill the King before they killed him? That wouldn't bring Gorget back. Should he invoke his escape clause now, and flee? Was there anything more to learn at this accursed court? What did Mab want from him? He turned to ask his friends what he should do, when he noticed that the formerly boisterous feasters had fallen silent.

The courtiers, including the King and Lilith, were, frozen in various attitudes, as if turned to stone. As Tom watched in amazement, the real inhabitants of the Scarlet Empire revealed themselves.

Little needle-tipped paws protruded from between the gaping mouths of all the seated figures, fastening upon the their lips. Flexing their arms, crimson lizards thick as fat snakes cracked the jaws of their human vehicles and poked their heads and half their bodies out. Wriggling, they emerged completely, hopping from their labial perches down upon the table. Standing on their hind legs, the lizards regarded the astonished visitors malevolently with beady eyes. Their tongues flickered in and out faster than a blink.

As one, the lizards bent quickly down, each scooping up a sharp dinner-knife. They leaped from the table to the floor, and began to advance on Tom and the others.

Tom emerged from his shock first. He whirled about, looking for Lug, who was behind him. Slowly the lizards began to encircle Tom and his friends.

"Lug!" Tom yelled. "Lug, where are you! Mab! Mab! Get us the hell out of —"

Book 3

7

The Black Demesne

"I'm never gonna do it
Without the fez on
Oh no
Don't make me do it
Without the fez on
Oh no
Please understand
That's what I am
I want to be your holy man"

         — Steely Dan, "The Fez"

"— here!"

Between the last two shouted words of Tom's invocation, everything changed.

The grim hall with its horde of disgorged menacing lizards vanished. Gone from Tom's vision was the traumatic sight of Gorget lying roasted upon the table. The

dusty red light and stifling heat of the Scarlet Empire
were lifted instantaneously from Tom's senses, and he
felt resurrected, like a groaning man declared prema-
turely dead, when the pall is drawn from his features by
the astonished mourners.

Still spinning from the impetus of his frantic search
for Lug (why did habit make him always look for Lug at
eye-level, despite the fact that the fachan barely came
up to his midriff?), Tom experienced only fragmentary
glimpses of blue sky, mild sun and something green.

Catching himself, he halted his dervish-like gyra-
tions.

It was late afternoon, and he was back at the Fork,
where red Road diverged from black. In the same
shocked attitudes they had held in the throneroom of the
Bastard King stood Natty and Nathan, blinking in the
unexpected light. The unflappable Lug, recovering first
from the transition, began to hop excitedly about the
trio, as if exceedingly proud of his role in their rescue.

Tracking Lug's exuberant leaps, Tom laid eyes on
their actual rescuer.

Mab had somehow erected a pavilion in their absence, smack in the middle of the Road. Despite the
rather dreary land around the Great Road at this
point — a morass full of cattails and sedge, reeds and
skunk-cabbage, contorted, desiccated tree-hulks —
Mab's retreat did not look out of place. Rather, by her
presence, she brought her reluctant surroundings into
congruence with her constructions. The world bowed to

her will and desires, as she re-formed what she would and invested the rest with a preternatural charm.

As if she occupied the middle of a fair pleasaunce with a full retinue of retainers and ladies-in-waiting, Mab reclined on a velvet couch under a billowing canopy of gauzy lime-green fabric upheld by silver poles. A carpet woven in a pattern of jade and white roses cushioned the clawed feet of her couch from the cobbles. A tripod beside her bore a tray piled high with fruit. Behind her a silver-bowled fountain in the shape of a boy riding a bulbous-nosed dolphin plashed and gurgled.

Tom had interrupted Mab's reading again. Apparently she still found much of interest in that same slim volume she had been perusing in the woods. This time, before Mab dismissed the book to its never-never-land, Tom caught its title:

Gold leaf on a spine of tanned leather: *Candide*.

The title meant nothing to Tom. With a twinge of disappointment, he dismissed it from his mind as just one more mystery connected with Mab that he was unlikely ever to penetrate.

Mab sat up. Her luxuriant platinum hair lay pooled for a second upon the couch as she lifted her head, looking like an alchemist's hoarded store of mercury. Strong, finely formed legs moved gracefully under her moss-colored kirtle as she swung them over the side of the chaise. Her delicately shod feet kissed the carpet. Resting her hands on either side of her hips, she hunched forward and regarded Tom and his companions with more than a hint of humor playing across her opaline lips.

Tom looked down at himself. His shoes were scorched and blackened, as if he had trod live coals. His bare calves were sooty, his tight pants grimy, and his capacious shirt smeared with remnants of his dinner with the King. His friends, he saw, looked no better, with the exception of Lug, who seemed somehow to keep himself naturally clean as a cat.

"You were hospitably received, I gather," said Mab.

Tom briefly considered getting angry with Mab, tried to work up at least a pale semblance of rage, failed, and, instead, smiled in his quirky way.

His perspective on life, it seemed, was coming more and more into line with that of the Faerie Queen. The longer he knew Mab, the less he was inclined to regard his life and actions in anything other than a lofty tragicomic fashion.

Which was not to say he wasn't a little irked with Mab, for several reasons. And this growing empathy with Mab on one hand, combined with an understandable human reluctance to recognize one's true stature in the uncaring universe, left Tom with a queer residue of emotion that baffled him.

But right now he couldn't find it in himself to complain.

"Seat yourselves," Mab invited. A wave of her hand summoned soft pillows around the legs of her couch. "Eat and drink, and tell me of what you saw."

Tom and Lug, Nathan and Natty, needed no further invitation. Each hefting several pieces of fruit, they fell gratefully down upon the cushions, like so many anxious suitors. Their stomachs were as mysteriously empty of the gruesome food they had so recently consumed at the hellish banquet as if it had been a phantom repast. Yet Tom still vividly recalled the taste of the colorless ichor that had flowed from the scorpion steaks. Had it all been a consensual illusion? If he had fallen from the snout of the castle, would he have died?

Regarding the charred leather of his buskins, and visualizing the havoc the Bastard King had wreaked on his cottage, Tom dismissed all thoughts that what he had gone through had been anything other than deadly real.

In between trips to the fountain — where he slaked himself with cool water dipped up in a silver cup that hung by its handle from a hook along the fluted rim — Tom told the whole story of his — days? months? years? — in the Scarlet Empire. When he was finished, Mab nodded wisely.

"Yes, that accords closely with what I witnessed through Lug, and with what I foresaw. You did well to call on me when you did, Tom. Whenever those puppet-masters forsake their human shells, they revert to primal instincts, and would have paid little heed to any injunctions I had placed on them to not to harm you."

"I'm glad I came back when I did, too," Tom said. "I don't think I could have learned anything more from that situation."

"Ah," said Mab, "that brings us to the meat of this nut. Nathan, Lug, Natty — please leave us now. Tom and I have something private to speak of."

The three so named rose up and moved off, Natty bowing elaborately to Mab before departing. He seemed quite recovered from the unimaginable embraces of the Red Queen, and his old sardonic self.

The sun was empurpling the west now, turning the scattered clouds overhead into indigo argosies freighted with dreams, sailing toward unguessable ports. Cooling as the sun disappeared, the late-spring air began to stir, the breeze like balm on Tom's limbs, especially after the smothering heat at the bottom of the pit. Peepfrogs began to chorus from the surrounding marshes, a plaintive sound.

Fatigue suddenly overtook Tom, enervating him and leaving him dizzy. He felt as if he had not stopped once since he had left Uncle Ross's farm. *When would he get some real rest?* he wondered.

Mab seemed to sense Tom's weariness. Patting her couch, she said, "Come, Tom, and rest beside me."

Tom stood, Mab slid up toward the head of the chaise, and Tom dropped tiredly down by her side.

To his immense surprise, Mab laid her hands upon Tom's shoulders and gently drew him back until he was lying with his head cradled intimately in her lap. Her delicious scent washed over him like easy combers on a sandy coast: jasmine and hyacinth, lilac and freesia, woodrose and carnation. Looking up he saw her downward-tilted face upside-down: delicate but determined chin, pearly lips, twin flared nostrils formed as delicately as the parts of some unearthly flower, and calm eyes grey as his own. Mab's hand came into view, and she began to stroke his brow. Tom gave a little start, recalling Mab's mark upon his jaw, and not wishing to have a similar moon-white forehead. But then he recalled that Mab had touched his bare hand also — before she spoke of Faerie — and had left no discoloration upon it. Apparently she could brand at will — or perhaps it had something to do with how she had deftly moistened her palm first with her feline tongue.

In any case, Tom relaxed and let Mab soothe him. It felt wonderful, and he almost fell asleep. But he knew that he still had something to discuss with this woman. Determined not to appear too malleable under her ministrations, Tom made an effort to chide her in a low-key fashion.

"Why didn't you tell me, Mab," Tom asked, "that I was going to meet the man who burned my house and tried to kill me and my mother?"

Mab continued to pass her chamois-soft hand over Tom's brow. "Would you have gone if you knew, Tom?"

Tom considered the question for a moment, wanting to give an honest answer. In the end, he could reply only with: "Maybe."

"'Maybe' would not have been good enough, Tom. You had to go, to learn what you have learned, and I was in no mood to argue with you, or strive to convince. I have told you I do not lie, Tom — although a liar could say the same, and still be consistent with his principles. But not to lie is not always to tell all of the truth. Someday you will see that there are times when charity and higher purposes compel silence in place of truth. Especially if one can speak nothing but."

Tom digested this. He remembered all the times he had bitten his tongue in the court of the Bastard King, instead of saying what he really thought. The notion was hard to accept — particularly for someone committed to finding out the truth about life — but Tom strove to integrate the idea into his view of the world.

Speaking slowly, Tom tried to get around the tollgate of the issue of honesty and back onto the high-road of the conversation. "Mab — what exactly was it that I learned? Or was supposed to learn?"

"You'll have to tell me, Tom."

Tom deliberated for a moment, choosing his words carefully.

"Well, back in the glade, I said I wasn't sure I knew anything about good and evil, and couldn't decide if Faerie was a path between the two. So I guess you were trying to give me closer look at evil."

Tom waited for confirmation, but Mab remained silent, although her hand still smoothed his black hair away from his eyes.

Tom spoke reluctantly, dragging each word up like a heavy bucket from a well. "I looked hard and long, Mab, and I still can't put into words what evil is. I guess I failed."

"Ah, but would you recognize evil again, Tom, whenever it appeared, in whatever guise it chose?"

Recognize the courtiers' cruel caprices and callous, offhand waste of life, the unique mixture of pride, stupidity and cunning that characterized the King and his Consort and their whole mad enterprise of visiting Hell? Of course he would, no matter what delusory and appealing raiments it wore.

"Oh, I'd recognize evil again, Mab. But is that enough?"

"For now," Mab replied, "that is quite an accomplishment, and all I ask of you. I think you've done remarkably well."

The praise excited Tom, more than any other words had ever done. Receiving Mab's benediction, he seemed to have taken a giant step forward toward his goal of a bright middle way. Her words conspired with the touch of her hand upon his brow, her sweet perfume and the feel of her thigh, to embolden him beyond anything he would have ever before dared.

Tom flipped over and sought to throw his arms around Mab's waist.

His chin hit the ground first, followed immediately by the rest of his body. Air shot from his lungs and a black and red veil danced briefly before his eyes. When he recovered from his impact with the cobbles of the Great Road, he sat up painfully.

Pavilion, couch, carpet, fountain and fruit had vanished as if they never were, an insubstantial pageant fading. Mab stood a few feet away, tapping one felt-shod toe, arms folded across her chest, as if waiting for Tom to stand.

Tom winced involuntarily, expecting to witness again the awesome transformation Mab had undergone the last time he had angered her. But she only stood with a look of amused impatience, and Tom at last got to his feet, wearing a sheepish look.

"In the morning, we'll discuss what's to come," Mab said.

Then she was gone.

At the instant of her uncanny departure, the sinking sun gave off the rare green flash regarded by Tom's old neighbors as an omen of upcoming miracles.

Tom wondered what further miracles he could expect — and tolerate — than what he had already undergone.

Picking up his scuffed wallet and scarred walking stick from where he had discarded them upon first being fetched back from the Scarlet Empire, Tom moved off to join his friends.

He found Natty, Lug and Nathan some distance off, huddling around a pile of damp, twisted branches they had gathered from the drier edges of the surrounding marsh. They were awaiting the application of Tom's steel and flint, but had not dared interrupt his interview with Mab.

Feeling chagrined that his friends had had to shiver while he dallied, Tom hastened to get the fire going.

When the damp wood had finally caught, everyone huddled close about the blaze to get warm, the marsh exhaling a thin miasma behind their backs, like a treacherous sycophant speaking ill of his lord when out of earshot.

Nathan spoke up first, after the chill had left their bones.

"Glad I am, Tom, that we escaped when we did from yonder evil red land. The Lord tested us in that furnace, and deemed us clean of soul. Had he not found us deserving, we would never have survived. And although I question not, I am puzzled about why one now among us was not doomed by heaven to remain behind and perish, so abhorrent were his actions."

Nathan looked with this last statement directly at Natty, who returned the preacher's glare with an insouciant smile that made him look foxier than ever.

"Listen, Silverprick, cast no aspersions about anyone's character until you've met and resisted similar temptations yourself. What does your stuffy tome say about throwing that first stone? I can't explain why I acted as I did in the place we visited. The very clods beneath my feet seemed to speak constantly to me of impossible riches and power just within my grasp. Yet now the whole affair seems a grandiose dream, similar to what I inevitably experience from too much dry sack and bad sausages. As for your precious Lord watching out for us — why, we owe our survival only to Tom's lady, who, I wot, is as far superior to your

Mosaic deity as a Queen is to a pox-ridden street-walker."

Nathan shot to his feet. "Blasphemy!" he shouted. "Take that foul lie back, you heathen, or I'll liberate your soul from your carcass, and send it straight to Hades!"

Natty was up and dancing about, like a butterfly drunk on pollen. The two men seemed ready to square off, before Tom and Lug intervened.

"Here now," Tom said. "That's no way to act. I assume we're to be companions for a while longer, and we must be tolerant of each other's views. Didn't we all fare well by sticking together in the Empire? If we're to travel the black Road tomorrow — as I suspect — then we'll need the same kind of camaraderie to get by."

Tom's speech appeared to have the desired effect, for the two men flattened their ruffled feathers (as did Lug, whose azure quills had literally erected themselves during the altercation, revealing a dusky aubergine hide), and settled down to a grumpy truce.

"All right," Nathan agreed. "But there must be no more insults about a man's religion."

"Or his personality," Natty chimed in.

"Good," said Tom. "Shake on it."

They did so, and settled down around the fire once again.

Natty seemed inclined to make amends. Reaching up one tattered sleeve, he miraculously withdrew the same pack of cards with which he had bamboozled Tom so long ago. Through chases and falls into dungheaps, fire and imperial assaults upon his body, Natty had somehow held onto the colored pasteboards.

"I know an intriguing game of chance, Nahum, that will reveal if the Lord is really on your side. I take three cards, two black, one red —"

"I don't gamble," said Nathan with finality.

Natty was about to let pass some caustic remark that might have re-started the fight when Lug motioned excitedly, thumping his chest with his gnarly fist.

"Aha," said Natty, "the monoped, at least, shows some fervor for an honest game. Who knows what supernatural favors he has to stake? I feel my luck turning for the better. Come closer, Lug, and I'll explain."

Lug nodded enthusiastically when Natty asked if the fachan had understood the details of the game. Then the play began.

Natty's long slender fingers whipped the cards through a circuitous flurry. Lug kept his huge eye fixed intently on the pasteboard hurricane. When Natty had finished, Lug unhesitatingly pointed to the middle card. Natty blanched and flipped it: the red.

The subsequent ten trials were all won by Lug. Natty had wagered a hypothetical quid he did not possess each time, and now stood severely in debt. With each loss, he had flinched a bit more deeply. Nathan watched, with barely concealed amusement threatening to crack his sober features, as did Tom.

Suddenly Natty snatched the cards up and deposited them back in their hiding place.

"Ha, ha," he weakly laughed. "I mentioned, did I not, Lug, that these first forays into teaching you the game were to have no pecuniary repercussions?"

Lug scowled, as if he had already planned how he was going to spend his eleven pounds. The thick, tombstone-like teeth of the fachan, which had never appeared threatening before, suddenly resembled the hungry grin of a manticore.

"All right, all right," said Natty. "I'll pay as soon as I am able. Although what an unlikely wight such as yourself will do with good mortal money is beyond my ken."

Lug's brow furrowed deeply, as if to say it was the principle of the thing.

Natty, grumbling, turned away and curled up to sleep. The others soon copied him in a less ill-tempered fashion.

Dawn came like the ghost of itself, the sun barely visible through the mists that had collected during the night. As Tom and the others stood and with aching muscles stretched, however, the solar disk began to burn off the haze, scattering the last shreds of it as a conquering army disperses its foes.

Tom found himself facing the wasteland that lay between the two arms of the Y. To his left, the red Road, a known quantity, arrowed. To the right, the as-yet untested black Road disappeared in the distance. And straight ahead —

Tom rubbed his eyes. Why couldn't he make sense out of what stretched away before him? One second, it looked like just more desolate fen: watery, tussock-dotted, eager to mire unwary travellers. The next second, the fen seemed to be an insubstantial illusion just barely preventing him from seeing something glorious that hid beneath.

He thought of asking the others what they saw, but knew from his earlier questioning that they would report nothing out of the ordinary.

A horse snorted behind him. Tom turned.

Mab straddled Endymion again, ready to see them on their way. She spoke to Tom.

"As you have no doubt guessed, Tom, it is your task now to travel the black Road, and learn from those who dwell along it. This time, I will warn you: the ruler of the land ahead is known to you. He it was who came upon you after the Bastard King left your house in ruins."

Tom's mind flashed back to the pumpkin-headed riders in black with their patriarchal liege, who had held him and his mother in the mud and storm. Should he hate this man more than the Bastard King, he wondered, as being directly responsible for Nora Rhymer's death? And yet, if the King hadn't come first, wouldn't Tom and his mother have been safe inside their intact home, and perhaps never even bothered? To assign responsibility for his misfortune seemed impossible, as causes and results and contingencies wavered fluidly in his brain. He resolved to enter this man's land with as unbiased a mind as possible, and make any decisions only after careful observation.

"All conditions from your first trip," continued Mab, "still apply to you and your friends. You can count on a grudging welcome, but little else. Fare carefully, Tom, and return safe to me."

Once more, Mab hawed Endymion around and rode away. As she cantered off, the bells braided into the horse's thick mane seemed to sound from leagues away, across sun-drenched fields unknown to man. Tom picked up his newly heavy satchel from the ground, gripped his stick and turned toward the black avenue.

Natty sniffed. "That haughty trull never even asked if Silverprick and I wanted to go this time."

"I guess she just knew," said Tom.

Natty considered this for a moment before saying, "Then I hope she divined exactly how sick I am of fruit."

Tom peered into his wallet, then looked at Natty with a smile.

"No one's omniscient."

Shortly after Tom hit the border of the Black Demesne, stopping as abruptly as if he had run into a brick wall, he felt as if someone had taken a straightedge, drawn a line down his middle, and neatly bisected him with a dull blade, in proof of one of Euclid's more obscure theorems.

After leaving the Fork that morning, Tom had asserted his leadership of the expedition by moving quickly to the front. He did not want to feel, as he had in the Scarlet Empire, that Natty (or anyone else, for that matter) was taking events out of his hands. Having seen how easy it was to be manipulated by forces beyond his understanding, Tom had resolved to exercise all his initiative and discernment, whenever confronted with a clear moral choice. He had let himself be buffetted by everyone else's whims for too long. Now he was going to direct his own affairs!

Natty did not contend with Tom for authority within the group. He seemed content to bound along on his lanky legs and whistle snatches of that cynical air about the country lout fleeced of his inheritance: "Taken to Market Like a Sheep."

Meanwhile, Nathan hung to the rear with Lug. The preacher whispered intently to the fachan throughout the hike. Lug seemed to regard the itinerant minister as an annoyance akin to an itch one could not reach. He tolerated the man's proselytizing as a horse might let a fly that couldn't bite crawl about its hide.

The going was fairly easy on this black branch of the Great Road. The fetid lowlands had fallen behind, to be replaced by a limitless lunar landscape much like the plain surrounding the Scarlet Empire: innumerable pebbles and rocks on a gritty soil — but no large boulders such as had hidden the hapless Gorget. Moreover, the sky was quite normal, both directly overhead and in the direction they travelled. No ominous tenebrous stripe of any color whatsoever lurked at the horizon.

All in all, Tom felt quite confident about getting through this part of his Mab-directed education with considerably less trouble than the first half.

After lunch and a brief rest they continued walking. So uneventful was their progress that Tom almost began to wish for something challenging to happen.

But when something did, it was nothing he was prepared for.

At an innocuous spot along the Road, in the interval between lifting his right foot up from the ground and setting it down again, Tom's sight underwent a radical derangement that halted him dead in his tracks.

The brief glimpse of an altered world he had gotten had made him shut his eyes as tightly as a coffin-lid. Slowly he pivoted on one foot, back toward his friends. Midway in his movements, he couldn't resist opening his eyes.

That was when the invisible geometer performed the bisection.

Tom's right eye was on one side of an intangible barrier, his left on the other.

Through his right eye, he saw the familiar world. There were his friends, standing puzzled at his apparently insane behavior. A bit past its apogee, the sun — insofar as he could look at it — was the same incandescent white-hot orb as ever. The small shadows each stone and pebble cast were an inky black.

Through his left eye, however, came the vision of a topsy-turvy world. Black and white seemed somehow reversed, all other colors shifted crazily along the spectrum. The sun was a jet blob in the grey sky, not a presence but an absence, a hole through which poured the cold void between worlds. The shadows in this land were white. Tom looked at his left hand: his skin was coal.

The antipathetic images coming through each eye merged in Tom's brain with shattering effect.

"*Gahhh*!" he moaned, shutting his eyes and crumpling to the paving.

Tom felt hands dragging him back along the Road's cobbles. He let them, all thoughts of taking the initiative forgotten. When his friends had hauled him a few feet back, he dared to open his eyes.

The mundane world returned his uneasy gaze.

Tom stood and feebly brushed himself off. Natty and Nathan were clamoring to know what had happened. As best he could, Tom described the sensation of having his vision split. Finishing, he said:

"Well, friends, what are we to do? Do we dare proceed into this land, where we can no longer rely on our most precious of senses?"

Natty stroked his nose, three fingers shading his lips, thumb under his chin. Nathan attempted to rub his eyebrow-mole entirely off. Lug just shifted uneasily from heel to toe of his big bare foot. Finally, Natty spoke, dropping his hand from his face.

"The trouble appears to have arisen from trying to take in two worlds simultaneously. I propose to venture beneath the black sun with my eyes closed, and only open them when fully within the queer land you describe."

Suiting his actions to his words, Natty strode bravely ahead, eyes shut. After about twenty steps he stopped and — back to the others — presumably opened his eyes. A slight jerk of his frame was the only evidence of consternation. Slowly he traversed a half-circle. He shouted out, "Friends, you and the world look most remarkable! But I experience no disabling seizure! Come join me!"

With trepidation, they did, making sure to keep their eyes tightly closed until entirely past the invisible interface.

Tom opened both eyes to the bizarre scene he had taken in with his left eye alone before. Natty had spoken truthfully; the human mind seemed to be able to deal with this derangement.

Tom saw that Lug was handling the sensual alteration without trouble. And as for Nathan —

The preacher had fallen to his knees and was weeping. Tom laid a hand on his shoulder. "What's wrong, Nathan? Are you in pain?"

Through his blubbering, the man said, "O, joyous day! The scales have fallen from my eyes! I have come unto the kingdom of the Lord!"

Tom looked dubiously around at the desolate inverted landscape. This was Nathan's conception of heaven? Was he himself missing something, or had the preacher gone mad? Tom raised the man up gently.

"We have to move on, Nathan. Whatever this place may be, we're supposed to meet its inhabitants, not linger in the wilderness. Let's go."

"Yes," said Nathan, "yes, we must meet the angels who inhabit this land."

Pulling away from Tom, Nathan stalked off down the Road, his long cape — now white — agitated by the force of his strides.

Tom saw his quest getting out of his control again, and hurried after him.

The other three caught up with Nathan and prevailed upon him to slow down. They continued their journey at a more sensible pace.

Now came further alarming changes.

Over the miles, a creeping cold began to infiltrate their ragged clothes. As if the black sun discharged a gelid wind along with its negative light, the air became bitterly chilled. Under the onslaught, Tom's teeth began to chatter, as did Natty's. Lug's quills fluffed up, like those of a bird in winter, as if to form a layer of insulating air.

Nathan, however, perhaps because of his heavy mantle, perhaps because of his apparently greater affinity for this land, seemed oblivious to the cold.

Remembering his blanket which had remained unused at the bottom of his scrip since leaving home, Tom dug out the rectangle of musty homespun wool. He and

Natty draped it over their shoulders and, like some awkward two-headed monster, shuffled together down the Road.

With the drop in temperature came a thinning of the air. As if they labored along the upper slopes of an alpine peak, they breathed strenuously, seeking to fill their lungs with the sparse atmosphere.

Eventually Tom called a halt. Nathan seemed quite willing and able to continue, but Tom and the others could hardly stagger on.

While they sat on the ground — each pebble was now rimed with black, which Tom knew in the real world he would see as white frost — a new startlement occurred.

Without warning, as if in compensation for their other troubles, their vision snapped back to normal.

Tom jumped up, pulling the blanket off Natty. That seated man was revealed as his old scarlet-clad self. Lug and the sky were blue, Nathan and the shadows black, the skin of the humans and the frost on the stones white. Still, an annoying tugging underlay Tom's vision, as if some part of his brain still struggled to deal with the black light which the sun must yet be pumping out.

Tom was about to ask Natty's opinion on what had happened — from the man's expression he knew they had shared the return to sensory normality — when the fellow volunteered it.

"I have read," said Natty, "of a doctor of philosophy — Galen or his like — who once performed an experiment upon a cat. He fitted the animal with a leather mask, in which were two lenses that distorted the world. At first the cat bumped into objects and generally navigated like a drunk. After a time, though, it seemed to perceive the world correctly, despite the lenses, making its way about as before. And when the doctor removed the mask, the cat went through the whole procedure again, first disoriented, later adjusting."

"And you think the same thing has happened to us?" asked Tom.

Natty shrugged, somewhat dispiritedly, and got to his feet. "Nothing else occurs to me. Do you think you might share that blanket again?"

Tom hurried to get Natty underneath the covering. "Oh, of course, I'm sorry."

Nathan, looking around the twice-altered landscape, still seemed borne up by some ecstatic transport. Seeing that the others had finished their rest, he moved off down the Road.

The four travellers walked on and on, through the dismal plain. Tom concentrated on getting the paltry air into his lungs and advancing one foot beyond the other. He and Natty were compelled to support each other beneath their common blanket, like two old men. Lug seemed also to have aged decades since they had entered the land of the black sun.

Tom studied the shadows of the pebbles strewn about him as he walked, finding it too much trouble to raise his head. Something was wrong about the shadows, even though they had regained their normal blackness. What was it?

Their size! thought Tom with a start. They were still of noontime smallness, although surely hours and hours had passed.

"Stop," Tom said. He looked up as the others halted.

The gloating sun still hung only a degree or two past its highest point. Behind its mask of whiteness it seemed to hide a nigrescent face.

"How are we going to know when to quit for the night," Tom said, "if there is no night?"

His friends regarded the motionless sun. Natty merely shook his head; Nathan, however, declaimed, "The Lord caused the sun to stand still for Joshua, and now for us! 'Tis a miracle indeed!"

"Oh, shut up," Tom said, instantly regretting it.

Nathan had not heard Tom, though, since he was staring intently off down the Road.

"At last," Nathan exclaimed, pointing, "the inhabitants of this blessed kingdom!"

Squinting his aching eyes, Tom could make out tiny figures in the distance. They must have just straggled over the horizon.

"Let's hurry," said Nathan, and set off.

Under the stationary hole in the sky, they advanced to meet the other party.

After a time, Tom could discern the nature of those they approached.

In the lead was a tall, thin man, barefoot and wearing

a shabby black robe. His head was massively deformed in the same way as those of the armored invaders who had once burst into Tom's life. An oblate spheroid, it made him look like a beanpole topped with a pumpkin. Some sort of device capped his squashed cranium.

Behind this figure came a group of children, all males about six years old, chained together.

The two parties met and stopped.

Raising a hand with palm facing, the man leading the children spoke.

"Greetings, pilgrims. You must be those who seek an audience with the Patriarch. All monks upon the Road were notified to watch for you, and aid you if we could."

Tom wanted to speak, but couldn't. His attention was riveted upon the man's head.

The device which the self-confessed monk wore like a cap was a heavy spoked wheel of wood, too small for an actual farm cart. On either side of the wheel was attached a notched metal strap. These straps met below the man's chin, and fed into a big padlock which apparently could slide up or down the notched straps, to regulate the tightness of fit.

The most repulsive thing about the arrangement was what it had done to the man's skull. Somehow, the rigid bones comprising the braincase had not been shattered by the compressive powers of the device, but rather molded. The man's skull swelled up to fill the interstices between the spokes. A hairy patch of skin even poked up from the axle-hole. The wheel looked as if it had been pressed horizontally downward into a gelatinous replica of the human head.

Tom found his voice, began to speak, squeaked instead, coughed to cover his confusion, found himself coughing for real, and had to be slapped on the back by Lug before he recovered.

Red-faced, Tom said, "Yes, that's us. We want to see the Patriarch. Will you take us there?"

"Certainly," said the man. "But first I must deliver these recruits to my monastery. As it lies in the same direction as the Tower, we will lose little time. Follow me."

The man set off down the Road, yanking on the chain leading to his charges to set them in motion.

The five boys, Tom saw, wore no wheels and had undeformed skulls like anyone else Tom had ever known. They sniffled as they walked along, chains clanking, but apparently did not suffer from the cold as much as the outsiders did.

Relinquishing his blanket entirely to Natty, Tom pressed on to the head of the coffle, wondering if the monk were going to lead them back all the way they had come. But even as he speculated, the man turned west at an unremarkable point and they set out across the cold desert.

What was the most polite way to broach the topic of the man's self-inflicted disfigurement? Tom was eager to learn what could have caused him to so severely mutilate himself, but hesitated to ask outright.

Settling upon an oblique approach, Tom said, "I am unfamiliar with the customs of your land. Perhaps as we walked, you might tell me something of the history of your community."

"Gladly," said the monk. "It is our sacred duty to enlighten all those who labor in darkness. First, know me to be John Gauntling, a ten-key monk of the Holy Order of Saint Fiune. And soon to be a fifteen-keyer, when these boys are delivered and begin their novitiate."

Gauntling's words caused Tom to notice the ring of keys that dangled from the cincture around the monk's waist. They seemed of a size to fit the chin-padlock Gauntling wore.

So much of what the monk said was confusing, that Tom didn't know what to ask next. He settled on mention of the unfamiliar saint.

"The glory of your order's patron has not reached me yet," Tom said. "Saint —"

Gauntling inscribed a circle on the fabric of his robe with a forefinger and looked to the heavens, as if piously offended at Tom's ignorance. "Saint Fiune, God rest his soul, should be known completely around this sorry world, if justice prevailed. But since we labor in a vale of tears, his faith and reputation spread slowly. Let me fill your ears with his glory, and so remedy at least a portion of this injustice.

"Many centuries ago, in the deserts of Syria, lived Saint Fiune. After a life of dissipation and waywardness, he was struck with the error of his ways, and retreated to the blazing sands to commune with the God he had so grievously offended.

"Wishing to be closer to the One Whom he sought to appease, he erected a tall column of stones he first hewed from the nearby cliffs with a spoon that never wore down, despite twenty years of quarrying. Then he ascended this pillar, vowing never to come down. Thus he became the first of those venerable martyrs known as Stylites.

"For the next fifty years, Saint Fiune lived upon the narrow compass of his pillar, surviving upon dew and manna vouchsafed him by the Lord. His days were filled with devotion, as were his nights, for no longer did he require sleep.

"Now, one day it chanced that beneath the holy man's column should pass the Emperor of Syria, a fierce and orgulous tyrant. He and his retinue were journeying somewhere, it matters not, and, as the Lord willed, their route took them by Saint Fiune's humble abode.

"Although already canonized by his own life, Saint Fiune was still a man, despite his abjuring of sleep and shelter. The dew and manna he consumed were mostly transubstantiated by his sacred bowels into pure sustenance. However, occasionally Saint Fiune found it necessary to micturate like you or me.

"For reasons we cannot fathom, the Lord caused the urinary impulse to diffuse from Saint Fiune's bladder to his brain just as the Emperor was standing below, marvelling at the spectacle of Fiune's devotion, which even his royally ignorant eyes could see. Fiune, dazzled by the desert sun and his holy thoughts, failed to observe the spectators below. Of a sudden, the Emperor's upturned face felt a holy yellow rain no desert skies had ever dropped.

"Spluttering with offended dignity, his wet face black with rage, the Emperor caused Saint Fiune's pillar to be hacked down immediately, toppling the Saint with it. One of the Emperor's massive war-chariots was brought forward, and Saint Fiune was lashed to one of its still attached wheels — not around the rim, as some urged, since the Emperor said that would be too easy an end, but across the diameter. Then the retinue departed the desecrated shrine.

"The sacred texts all tell us that Saint Fiune survived the journey back to the Syrian capitol, and, in fact, the next twenty years of nearly constant rotation as he accompanied the Emperor whenever that monarch took his chariot out for a spin. Doubtlessly, Saint Fiune would be with us to this day, had the chariot he was bound to not plunged over a cliff during battle, into a bottomless ravine.

"Our order arose soon after, eventually settling far from the Holy Land, in this northern wilderness. In memory of Saint Fiune, we each wear a miniature wheel upon our heads, as you perhaps have noticed."

Tom, awed by the long and improbable tale, nodded numbly, to indicate that this little matter had not escaped him.

"Of course," continued Gauntling, "not everyone in our land has taken holy vows. We have several villages where the laity live. I have just come from one such, where I recruited these children for our order. And although there is a sisterhood complementary to our order, they do not wear the wheel, since Saint Fiune's pronouncements are plain about the proper role of women, those carriers of original sin. Additionally, there is one man among us who need not don the wheel to signify his holiness. That is our Patriarch. He is an actual contemporary of Saint Fiune's, the living founder of our order. Touched by the hand of the martyr himself one day, as Fiune's chariot rolled through the marketplace, our Patriarch was instantly converted, and endowed with the years of Methuselah, so that he could guide our order."

Gauntling's long speech had helped to pass the weary miles across the trackless waste. Now Tom looked away from his guide to see a squat building of black bricks sitting some distance off, like an immense toy block discarded by a giant's petulant child.

"The monastery," Gauntling said. "Now I add to my keys."

8

The Stern Patriarch

"What is God but a despairing refutation of Man?"

— Ben Hecht, *Fantazius Mallare*

The bricks of the monastery were glazed black. They seemed to soak up the light of the eye-boggling sun, hoarding and concealing it as a miser sits upon his coins or a murderer locks up within his breast the secret knowledge of his crime.

Through the arched door passed first Tom and John Gauntling, followed by the dazed and ill-clothed children trailing their chains, with Natty, Lug and Nathan tailing along behind.

Tom had hoped that the building would offer some protection from the cold of the desolate plain through which they had so arduously labored. Perhaps, he thought, its bricks had absorbed same heat from the ever-present sun, and would radiate it upon the inhabitants. His hope died a quick death as soon as he entered the windowless structure. Inside, it seemed even colder than without, a piercing frigidity that dulled his brain and limbs. It was as if they entered an icehouse. He wondered how the barefoot monk and the boys could stand the hyperborean climate. Either their spirituality must render them insensible to the cold, or they must have icewater in their veins.

Another monk greeted them in the large, bare room just beyond the entryway. Shoeless on the ebony tiled floor, robed and wheel-capped, he bore a generic resemblance to Gauntling. Perhaps twenty years older, he differed mainly in that his skull was even more compressed than the cranium of the monk who had led Tom and his friends here.

When the second monk saw them, he signed himself on his chest with the circle symbol and said, "Praise God, Brother Gauntling! I see you have succeeded in your mission to bring new souls into the order. At the investiture later, I will be proud to tighten your straps. Nine candidates is an exemplary accomplishment. If they live, that will make you a nineteen-keyer, second only to Odobert."

The new monk regarded Tom with evident calculation as to what size wheel he would wear. When his eyes fell on Lug, he started and then glared at Gauntling. "What subterfuge is this, Brother Gauntling? Surely you know we do not accept such creatures into the order."

"Praise God and Saint Fiune," Gauntling replied. "Heaven has indeed smiled on me, but not to the extent you believe. Only the five youths are candidates for the order. These other four strangers are those we were told of, who go on to the Tower and the Patriarch."

"So your ring will hold only fifteen keys at most," said the other monk. His hand dropped unconsciously to his own ring, and caressed the dangling keys. (Tom estimated they must number between fifteen and twenty.) The somber face of Gauntling's apparent superior barely disguised an alarming degree of proud gloating. "Well, still and all, a fine end to your mission, Brother. I'm sure you'll want to rest now. There is an empty cell down the hall from yours — Brother Clothard was called to the Test just yesterday. The visitors may rest there, before the investiture, which I am sure they will wish to attend." The second monk left after giving these directions, hurrying through one of the inner doors.

Gauntling turned to Tom and said, "Brother Benedict was responsible for my own entry into the order, and consequently holds my key. Naturally he takes a commensurate interest in my spiritual progression."

"I see," said Tom, between teeth that clicked as noisily as cicadas in a heatwave.

Gauntling led them out of the anteroom and down several cold corridors. The cells of various monks — doorless and plain to view — opened off the corridors. Tom could see the community at rest, its members lying on their hard beds, wearing their wheels and studying books that must contain the words of Saint Fiune. The cells were all identical, and Tom felt after a time that he was passing and re-passing the same one continuously.

At last their guide stopped at an empty chamber. "This is your room," he said. "Mine is just a few doors down, on the opposite side. If you need me, I will be there as soon as I hand over these lucky boys to the Brother in charge of the ceremonies."

Gauntling left Tom and company to investigate their new quarters on their own.

There was not much to see. A simple table held a crock of water and a bowl of thin wafers. On one wall hung a diptych depicting Saint Fiune first on his pillar, then bound upside-down on his wheel. A narrow bed of boards held a folded robe at its foot. This habit Tom donned, in an only partially successful attempt to evade the cold. Natty continued to huddle under Tom's blanket, while Lug had the comfort of his quills. Nathan seemed indifferent to anything beyond the confines of his fevered brain, which — if the beatific expression on his horsy face was any gauge- — was filled with haloed angels and the sound of the Final Trump.

Tom sat down wearily on the edge of the disagreeable bed. Lug joined him with evident relief, his lone foot swinging a few inches above the black tiles of the floor. Nathan paced about the room, filling the empty air with frequent hosannas. Natty moved slowly to the low table, then returned to sit on the bed, bearing the crock and bowl in his hands. Tom, Natty and Lug passed the water among themselves; then, as if celebrating some obscure communion, they fell greedily upon the wafers.

The dishwater-colored circles tasted like paste and seemed to coat the tongue and roof of Tom's mouth. Still, they represented a possible source of energy the travellers felt much in need of, so they chewed and swallowed diligently, albeit without enthusiasm.

When their tasteless meal was finished (Nathan had ignored their offer to share in it), Tom and his bedmates remained sitting, pressing closer together to conserve their body heat, and fell into a kind of fitful upright half-sleep.

After an indefinite period of shivering rest, Gauntling the monk returned and roused them. He was carrying a flagon that brimmed with a thick milky liquid.

"Pardon me," said Gauntling, "if I do not offer you any of my drink. It is that elixir known as *siqoqtoaq* and I must consume this amount and more before the investiture, if I am to be ready. I do not think you would relish its effects, unless you had committed yourself to become one of us."

Tom eyed the noisome liquid. The wafers he had so laboriously ingested threatened to rise up into his throat.

"Just as well," Natty offered, "for the meal we have recently consumed was all we could handle."

Gauntling quaffed deeply from the goblet, wiping his lips afterwards with a sleeve. "Already I can see that the example of Saint Fiune's fifty years in the desert has had the beneficial effect of moderating your fleshly appetites. I am certain that the sermon we are about to hear shall have a further salutary influence on your behavior. Let us go now to the chapel."

Tom gripped the hallucinating Nathan by the elbow and made sure the preacher accompanied them without dashing off in pursuit of some vision and getting lost. Gauntling brought them shortly to the chapel.

The big room's ceiling was two stories above their heads. Rows of comfortless benches held ranks of monks, each kept apart from his neighbors by the diameters of their wheels. Hung on the wall facing the benches was a lifesize representation of Saint Fiune upon his spoked torture bed. In front of this *memento mori* stood an unadorned lectern, beside which sat the five boys whom Gauntling had carried away from their homes and across the frosty plain to the black monastery. Empty goblets lay at their feet, and their upper lips were frosted with white. They looked utterly dumbfounded and powerless.

Gauntling led Tom and his friends to an empty bench and bade them sit. Nathan did so only reluctantly, appearing to prefer chasing angels through the empty air, perhaps hoping to cajole them to dance on the pins and needles Tom was beginning to feel in his extremities.

Clutching his borrowed robe more closely about him, Tom waited for the sermon to start. Lug looked as if for the first time in his life he wished he had two arms, with which to hug himself warmer. Natty had his blanket up over his head, hiding his carroty hair as in a hood.

A monk with a particularly oblate skull, carrying well over twenty keys at his belt, emerged from a side door and proceeded to the lectern. Gauntling had just enough time to whisper "Brother Odobert" to Tom, before the sermon began.

"Our topic today, Brethren," said Odobert, "is bricks.

"Consider the humble brick. It starts its useful life as a formless, undifferentiated mass of clay and water. Without the intervention of Man, it would remain such until the earth crumbled into dust. But Man does intervene in the passive life of this clay. He scoops it up from the riverbank, perhaps, or digs deeply for veins of it underground. Then he packs what he has sundered from the ground into a mold, smoothing off its top to accord with his plans. Knocked out of its primal mold, the brick rests for a time amid straw, with its cousins turned out by other hands. Then Man selects the best bricks from their nest and bakes them, along with others of their kind, in fierce ovens precisely fired and carefully tended.

"At last the brick is finished. Or is it? Take a closer look at this brick, Brethren. What color is it? Red!

"Red as blood, red as sin! Is this a fit color for an object that will be dedicated to the glory of God, in the Tower a-building out upon the plain? Of course it is not! Throw out this faulty, offensive brick, Brickmaker, and try again. This time, use all your ingenuity and concoct a glaze, a glaze of a holy color. Black! Black as the night that was good enough for God before he declared, 'Let there be light!' Black as the souls of men, as a reminder of what we must purge from ourselves. Anoint new bricks, this time with the sacred glaze, and submit them again to the furnace. What have you now? A shining black brick, fit for a holy Tower.

"Do I need to belabor my allegory, for ears that will hear it? We have strangers in our midst today, as you have noticed, travellers from a benighted realm, and so I will spell everything out, lest their deaf ears hear not.

"Man started his life as a shapeless mass of clay and water, which God separated from the earth and formed in His own image. The primal mold was Eden, which God destined Man to lose, The straw in which Man nestled for a time — and in which the flawed bricks still remain — is the outside world, with all its petty knavery and temptations. The curative oven is our monastery, wherein Man is purified and hardened. And just as we hide our shameful bloody innards within our white skin, so do we further conceal these also despicable hides within robes of pure black.

"What of the edifice that is to be built out of human bricks? That is the invisible temple of daily devotion. Each of us is a brick in that magnificent structure. And although there is no gainsaying that the physical Tower is a splendid tribute to the Lord, remember that the invisible structure is just as grand.

"Now, holding this lesson firmly to our bosoms, let us pray."

Odobert emerged from behind the lectern and dropped to his knees. All the monks followed suit, and Tom felt it best to comply with the form, if not the spirit of the activity.

On his knees, Tom wondered if any of these monks had been among those who had held him down in an identical posture so many, many days ago, in what seemed like another life.

The interminable silent mediation finally ended, and everyone resumed their seats, small improvement over the cold floor. Odobert approached the stupefied boys — who had remained seated — and laid a hand on the softening head of one of them.

"O, Saint Fiune," he intoned, "today we consecrate five more souls to your glory. Just as you suffered for twenty years upon the wheel, so do we signify our devotion to you by fastening the wheel upon our own brows. Thanks to that sovereign elixir revealed to the Patriarch in a dream, *siqoqtoaq*, our skulls alone of all our bones are made malleable, to bear the living impress of your burden. Thus do we testify more and more sincerely with every passing year. These five youths at first will bear but little pressure from their new crowns. Yet be patient, Saint Fiune — soon they will show the world the full extent of your pain!"

With a motion, Odobert called forth five young keyless monks who each carried a wheel-cap for one designated boy. The wheels were placed upon the heads of the unresisting drugged boys. One by one, Odobert gathered up the notched metal straps beneath each chin and slipped them through the locking device, shoving the big padlock up firmly into the soft flesh of the underjaw and twisting a key within to lock it. The wheels sank just perceptibly into each skull. Removal was impossible.

Odobert straightened when the investiture was over. "Now, let Brothers Gauntling and Benedict come forth."

The two monks left their seats and stood in front of their peers. First Odobert added the five keys to Gauntling's ring. Then he expertly palpitated Gauntling's gourd-like skull while Benedict looked on proudly. The head monk announced, "Brother Gauntling, the *siqoqtoaq* has worked so well in you that I deem you may advance a full two notches!"

Gauntling quivered in obvious joy at being so exalted. Benedict selected a key on his ring, removed it and inserted it in Gauntling's lock. Then, firmly grasping Gauntling's two straps, he pulled.

The lock slid up one notch with an audible *click*! Down came the wheel, further compressing a skull that already seemed at the limits of its permissable distortion. Tom, who had almost fallen asleep during the ceremony, was now wide awake. He winced as Gauntling's head was squeezed. Surely they would not try another notch —

Benedict did.

Gauntling stumbled back to his seat with an indescribable look of mingled agony and pride written across his flattened face. He seemed to want to say something to Tom, but apparently found it impossible to speak.

"Services are over," declared Odobert. "Our visitors may return to their cell. When Brother Gauntling is fully recovered, he will have the honor of conducting them to the Tower."

Tom, Natty, Nathan and Lug left the chapel.

Back in their room they found the food bowl refilled with wafers.

But no one felt like eating.

What distinguished a minute from an hour, an hour from a day, a day from a year? Tom pondered this question with all the resources his tired mind could muster. Obviously, they were all units of time, just as ounces and pounds were measures of weight. The difference was one of size; that much seemed clear. But what was size? Was there such a thing as absolute size? Wasn't size a relative matter? What was small in one context might be large in another. And if an observer had only one thing within range of his senses, could he assign a size to it at all? Without a reference point or second object for comparison, what seemed to be a mouse might be as large as an elephant.

Tom had no way of knowing if their passage across the frigid plain, after leaving the monastery, had taken them mouses or elephants. The black sun hung at its perpetual zenith as they trudged across the barren earth,

plodding with heads down, following Brother Gauntling, who seemed to know where they were going. At
random intervals they stopped for water and wafers and
a bit of rest. Then the whole ordeal began again.

They were moving slowly across the vast vacancy
when Tom suddenly experienced a sudden partial failure
of his vision. Either that, or the light of the queer sun had
diminished. Tom lifted his heavy head and saw that he
had crossed the edge of an enormous shadow. Raising
his eyes still further, he found himself staring at the
Tower.

The cylindrical building stretched up into the cloud-
less sky so high that Tom was unable to see its top. Black
as midnight, it seemed a cruel spear thrust from heaven
into the ribs of the earth. Tiny figures swarmed around a
series of petty outbuildings at its base.

"We're almost there now," Gauntling encouraged
them. He had regained the power of speech not long ago,
although his jaws barely moved when he spoke and it
was sometimes hard to comprehend him. Perhaps addi-
tional draughts of *siqoqtoaq* would elasticize his mouth
and restore his former eloquence. But for now, further
stories of Saint Fiune — or anyone else — were not in the
offing.

"How — how big is that thing?" Tom asked.

"Three thousand cubits across the base, and half
that number tall," answered Gauntling. "But we're still
building."

Tom did a mental conversion. The structure was

roughly a mile in diameter and half that in height. It was as impossible a thing in its way as the pit in the Scarlet Empire. In fact, Tom realized — with a strange sensation as if his brain were a half-cooked johnnycake and someone had just flipped it — this Tower was really a mirror-image counterpart to that gigantic excavation.

"Let's get there as soon as possible," Tom said, fearing he knew what awaited them.

Soon they were among the comparatively small buildings that clustered, in reality, far from the base of the Tower. The structures were huge kilns, piles of firewood brought from who knew where stacked beside them, and mingy huts for the laborers, who were wheelless lay folk.

Working his strapped jaw with painful concentration, Gauntling seemed compelled to pass on the glorious history of the Tower that hung over them like a perpetually falling mountain.

"When the Patriarch first came to this land with his small band of followers, centuries ago, they were met by an unclean female spirit who guarded the place. Confronting the faithful, she was an alluring succubus with hair the color of platinum. Immediately the Patriarch and his followers dropped to their knees and began an exorcism. The ritual must have worked, for the spirit finally vanished. But before she did so, she called out, 'Foolish men, you'll get no closer to Heaven by coming here.'

"So angered was the Patriarch that he proclaimed that on the very spot where the spirit had mocked them, he would build a Tower stretching to the Lord's very throne."

The small speech had exhausted Brother Gauntling, and he kept silent until they stood at last at the very wall of the Tower. So gradual was its curve that it almost seemed they confronted a flat surface. Built into the outer wall was a wide ramp leading up. All along the base, workers loaded pallets with bricks, which, at pre-arranged intervals, were hoisted up in swings. Other workers trundled barrows full of mortar up the ramp.

Tilting his head back, Tom strained to see the top, but only grew dizzy. The Tower seemed to narrow as it ascended.

"The Patriarch," Gauntling informed them, "lives on the highest floor — which is superseded every few years — with a few of his holiest disciples. The lower floors are filled with those who construct and maintain the Tower, as well as the militant monks of our order, who defend our realm against the depredations of a vicious fiend known far and wide as the Bastard King."

"The name is familiar," Tom said. "I don't suppose we could ride one of those slings to the top."

"Impossible. It would set the construction schedule back by precisely one load of bricks."

Tom set a foot upon the ramp. "I have an idea this will take some time. Shall we get going?"

"Your zeal is admirable," Gauntling said.

Tom just shook his head and began to climb.

In a span of time denominated fancifully by a whole

Hannibal's troop of elephants later, they reached the summit, muscles aching, lungs working like the bellows on the brick-kilns below to extract the barest sufficiency from the rarefied air. Down from above filtered the sounds of construction. Looking up, Tom saw a nearby load of bricks arrive at the end of a long swinging boom that thrust far out to compensate for the Tower's inward slope from bottom to top.

Facing Tom and his weary friends was a door leading inside.

Gauntling took them through it.

Tom found himself in a vast room that echoed with their footsteps. Its shape was that of a truncated pie-piece, at its far end a barely visible dot of a door. Along its slanting walls of glazed brick were stapled those curious torches Tom had first seen when the black riders arrived at the ruins of his home. These flares seemed the product of some subtle alchemy, for they never flickered or dwindled, but burned with a constant harsh glare that stung the eyes and made all shadows into suspiciously independent, knife-edged skulkers.

The room was empty, and no one waited to conduct them to the Patriarch. Remembering the lengthy parade of warriors who had flanked the Bastard King, Tom had expected a similar display here. He asked Gauntling, "Where are those militant monks you spoke of? Doesn't the Patriarch require an honor guard?"

"Those Brothers who don armor when duty calls are required to make a supreme sacrifice. In order to fit into their helmets, they must remove their wheels. The consequent relaxation of cranial pressure, and the public diminishment of years of sacrifice, are so unsettling that the Brothers fight particularly savagely and quickly, so as to return and be refitted with their sacred crowns. As you might suspect, under such conditions ceremonial wearing of a warrior's gear is not practical. Also, our Patriarch does not rely on such shows as you are familiar with to shadow forth the grandeur of his being. His person alone indicates his spiritual depth."

Gauntling's jaw must be loosening up, thought Tom. If he had known he was going to provoke such a lecture, he would have held back on his questions.

Taking a deep breath of the unsatisfyingly thin and chilled air, Tom said, "I am most anxious to meet the founder of your order."

This was only the truth, Tom felt, since the sooner he was finished here, the sooner he could return to Mab.

Gauntling almost smiled. "I too long to be once more in his austere yet magnificent presence. Follow me."

The five set out down the roughly trapezoidal hall.

As they walked, their mixed shod and bare soles slapping on the tiles, Gauntling — his jaw hinges finally well-oiled by the constant applications of *siqoqtoaq* he had taken as they crossed the plain — continued to inform them of the Tower and its inhabitants.

Tom listened only half-heartedly, his mind and body fatigued from the upward spiral journey.

"Each floor of the Tower is laid out," said Gauntling,

"as a wheel. This room and its counterparts along the rim make up the spokes. At the center is a circular room corresponding to the hub of the wheel. The hub on this top floor is the Patriarch's throneroom. This spoke of the holy wheel is a formal antechamber, whereas the others are quarters for those who enjoy the daily presence of our Patriarch.

"Should you wish to address our Patriarch by one of his many titles, be advised that the one he most prefers is 'He Who Holds All Our Keys.' This appellation refers to the fact that the Patriarch holds the Master Key to all our locks. At any time he may, if he so choses, elevate one of us poor monks by as many notches as he sees fit."

A look of mixed dubiety, alarm and joy passed over Gauntling's flattened face. "Thus it is advisable for those who visit the Patriarch to have plenty of *siqoqtoaq* mixed with their other arterial humours, in case he decides one is worthy of having his straps cinched."

For a time Gauntling was silent, as if the prospect of further advancement required much contemplation. When he spoke again, it was on a different subject.

"This floor is newly occupied," said the monk. "Now the Patriarch and his court are that much closer to the Heaven we all seek. Of course, this is occasion for the Test. Perhaps you recall that the cell you briefly occupied back at the monastery once belonged to Brother Clothard, who was summoned hither to participate in the Test."

Tom recalled no such thing, but he nodded yes anyway.

"Well," Gauntling said, "Brother Clothard was only two or three days ahead of us in his journey to the Tower. He may yet be preparing himself for his *auto da fe*, and it could be our luck to witness his act of supreme devotion."

Tom was about to ask what the Test consisted of, when Gauntling stopped. They had come to the door set into the convex wall at the far end of the anteroom.

Gauntling said, "Make ready to enter the presence of the holiest man on our imperfect earth."

Gauntling conducted Tom and the others with awe into the hub of the monastic universe.

The large round room was filled with barefoot, black-robed monks sitting or standing in various poses of reverent meditation. Some stood on their heads, their wheels serving as stable bases, so as to apply extra cranial pressure in a holy manner. The pitiless torches lit the skinny forms of the monks with an unnerving radiance akin to what inconceivable creatures of flame dwelling on the very sun might experience. In the center of the room was a circular platform, atop which was a craggy ebony throne looking as if it had been cleaved from a mountaintop and set down with minimal finishing. This rude chair held the giant form of the Patriarch.

His stern face — that small portion around the eyes and nose not concealed by his thick, white, chest-long beard — was as Tom remembered it from the long-ago

night: an implacably devout and uncompromising
visage. A feature hidden that night was the flowing
white hair that fell to his shoulders. The man's black
robe caused the rest of him to blend into his throne, as if
the two of them had been fashioned from the same rocky
stuff. His massive hands alone emerged from his sleeves,
clutching a giant key in his lap, symbolic of the real
master opener that hung from his cincture.

Seated on cold stone at the bare feet of the Patriarch
was the first woman Tom had seen among the monks.

Her head was utterly normal, its virginally perfect
curves revealed by the close cropping of her black hair,
which was as short as a field newly reaped. Her skin was
white as chalk, her face as demure and unself-conscious
as a child's. Her willowy body was clothed in black; legs
bent beneath her, her slim bare feet rested against her
thin haunches. When she spied Tom looking at her, she
lowered her eyes bashfully to her folded hands that were
clasped as if in prayer.

Closer now to the dais, Tom moved to the head of his
party to offer greetings to the Patriarch. He had barely
opened his lips when Nathan rushed past Tom and
threw himself down upon the Patriarch's bare feet,
which he began to kiss.

"O, Lord," Nathan moaned between kisses, "Thou
hast seen fit to rapt me up to Thy Heaven, to sit forever
beside Thee. My life of travail is over. O, all praises unto
Thee, Host of Hosts —"

Many of the monks had ceased their devotional

activities and turned with shock to the transgressing Nathan. Fearing the appearance of those wicked crossbows he had once had trained on him by the black warriors, Tom hastened to drag Nathan off the Patriarch, who had not moved throughout the display of adoration.

Once Nathan was hauled away from the kiss-be-slobbered feet of the Patriarch, he suddenly stiffened in Tom's arms. His eyeballs rolled up into his head and he collapsed to the floor, victim of his Apollonian fervor.

Leaving Natty and Lug to tend to the stricken preacher, Tom tried to recover something from the disrupted audience. "He Who Holds All Our Keys," Tom said nervously, "we are honored that you have consented to receive us. Allow me to offer you a token of the faith that exist in the world outside your Demesne."

Tom scrabbled in his wallet for the book he had also offered to the Bastard King — or rather, that half of it which survived. Luckily, Paradise remained intact, and would certainly please the Patriarch.

The Patriarch took the offered book from Tom's trembling hand, still without a word. He read a page or two with excruciating slowness, then looked up.

"Bring me a torch," he said in stentorian tones.

Tom assumed that the aged Patriarch was having trouble seeing the small print — although how the room could be any more brightly lit, he did not know.

The torch came, carried by a wheel-capped monk.

The Patriarch, big key now resting in his lap, took the flare in his free hand. Bending forward, he laid the book down at his feet, away from the woman seated there. Then he applied the torch to it.

The book practically exploded into cold flames. Tom watched in amazement as it burned away to nothing, leaving not even a flake of grey soot upon the black dais. The last remnant of the volume that had once obsessed him was gone, as if it had never been. Tom suddenly felt as if all those vanished chapters signified the close of some final chapter in his own life.

"We need no outside revelations, for these be heresy," said the Patriarch, handing the torch back to the waiting monk and gripping his key again. "The words of Saint Fiune alone suffice unto eternity."

Tom was totally lost for a reply. He couldn't find it in his heart to repudiate Master Alighieri (whose work he had once so dearly loved, even while admitting it did not hold the answer to all his questions). Yet he felt constrained to appease the Patriarch, lest the stern man put them all to some unimaginable inquisition.

An interruption saved Tom the necessity of formulating some ameliorative, yet truthful speech. Rushing in from one of the many doors around the periphery of the room, a monk arrowed down the radius to the Patriarch's throne. He fell upon his knees and hung his burdened head, saying, "Forgive me, Lord, but I bring news of grave import. Brother Clothard — he who was nominated for the Test — has succumbed to the cinching you honored him with."

A hush filled the chamber. Beneath his rug of a beard, the Patriarch's invisible lips seemed to twitch uncontrollably. The silence stretched as long as the distance from the tip of an elephant's trunk to the end of its tail. At last the Patriarch spoke:

"Arise, messenger, and receive thy due."

The monk stood on rubbery knees and stepped upon the dais. The Patriarch lifted his ring bearing the master key and inserted the skeleton device into the monk's lock.

With one savage pull he racheted the lock three notches.

Click-click-click!

The monk clutched his blessed head, howled and fell to the floor, to be carried away by his brethren.

Tom was quivering in his boots with anger, cold, and fear. Regarding the seated ruler of this black land with a deep loathing, Tom was somehow reminded of the Bastard King. Although the two men could have not been more different in their looks or demeanors, they struck him as two sides of the same coin. Piety and impiety, control and rage, austerity and indulgence, beneficence and cruelty, Heaven and Hell — these opposites seemed separated by only the smallest layer of base metal, a coin worn thin by much handling.

Only Natty and Lug rushing to his side prevented Tom from ending his rigid paralysis by doing something wild that would have doomed them all.

"I must retire," said the Patriarch in frosty tones, "to contemplate who shall take the place of Clothard in the Test. His spirit was willing, but his flesh was weak."

A chorus of "Amens" filled the room.

The Patriarch indicated with a wave the woman seated at the base of his throne. "This is Mariam, most devout of all my holy daughters of the spirit who dwell in the cloisters below. She shall show the pilgrims to a chamber where they may pass their time in prayer, until called to witness the Test."

Mariam rose gracefully, with an air of utmost humility, as if undeserving of the kind phrases of the Patriarch. Still with downcast eyes, she moved away from her spiritual father, toward one of the doors leading from the hub.

Tom and Natty picked up the unconscious form of Nathan and, with Lug following, set out across the waste of black tiles behind Mariam.

As they neared the concave wall and one particular door, Tom heard the Patriarch boom out:

"Brother Gauntling, approach the throne — !"

Then they were out of the throneroom, and in one of the spokes.

This corridor was narrower than the other, and lined with arches which, Tom saw, led to sparsely furnished cells. At the far end was a small speck of daylight. From what he remembered of his long ascent, Tom was fairly certain that the exterior ramp did not come close to any other door that opened at this level. The arch at the end of this spoke must debouch onto sheer air, half a mile above the stony ground.

Midway down the corridor, Mariam halted. She raised her meek eyes to Tom, who found himself instantly entranced by them. The purity and sanctity that shone in her doe-like eyes, and in every ivory plane of her virginal face, was like nothing he had ever experienced. His pulse began to race, and his consciousness threatened to dissolve in a white blaze of respectful adoration. The opposite of carnally seductive, this creature yet managed to seduce Tom's mind and soul with the promise she offered of attaining perfect bliss. Her bloodless lips, parting gently, seemed ready to drop words of revelation like the rain of manna that had kept Saint Fiune alive for so long.

Mariam said only, "Here may your red devil of a friend wait. Bid him enter hurriedly, for he affrights me."

Tom turned to Natty as if mesmerised. "Natty, wait here," he said haltingly.

Natty, clutching his blanket around himself, sized Tom up with a look of concern. But in the end — whether from tiredness, confusion, or respect for Tom's independence — he said nothing, and simply went into his doorless cell.

Mariam conducted Tom — who now carried Nathan with Lug's help — to the next cell. "Lay your holy man here to recover," she said. "The splendor of our Patriarch will leave him insensible for a while yet."

Lug and Tom arranged Nathan on the cushionless bunk within. Mariam said, "Tell your underworld creature to remain here, to watch over the sleeper."

"Lug, stay here with Nathan," Tom repeated.

Lug seemed to ache for a voice with which to protest, but finally did as Tom ordered.

Mariam left with Tom. Out in the long corridor, they found themselves entirely alone.

"You are dressed in the holy color," Mariam said, indicating Tom's borrowed habit as they moved on. "And I sense a deep urge within you to learn about Heaven."

"Yes," Tom agreed soporifically. "Yes, I must learn about Heaven. I've already been to He —"

Mariam cut Tom off, as if what he had been about to utter was not fit for her ears.

"I can teach you," Mariam said, coming closer to Tom. Without actually touching him, she seemed to insinuate tendrils of possession into his soul. Her odor drifted to Tom, a smell like parchment and the bitter incense from thuribles.

"Come pray with me in my room," offered Mariam. "Together we will achieve enlightenment."

They continued down the corridor, finally coming to a cell that Mariam identified as her own. Inside, Mariam indicated that Tom should kneel upon a well-worn prayer-rug. He did, and she positioned herself beside him.

"Before we begin," Mariam said, "I must ask you a question. You seemed about to assert just now that you had visited that very place which our Savior once harrowed. Can it be true?"

"No, not the very place," said Tom, refraining from naming Hell in front of Mariam, as the word seemed to disturb her. "But a place very much like it, ruled by one called the Bastard King."

Mariam signed herself with the wheel, and gave a charming little shiver of fear. She seemed tantalized by the subject, like a scared child who — despite his fear — insisted on his parent continuing with a ghastly tale.

"Our dreaded foe. He raids the Black Demesne from time to time, slaughtering and pillaging until our warriors drive him off. He and our Patriarch have never waged single combat, you know. Whenever one appears on the battlefield, the other is absent. It is said — by those who explicate such things — that they have never met yet because God has not willed it. Should they ever stand face to face, so the doctrine has it, it will signal Armageddon, and the world will end."

Tom nodded intelligently, captivated more by the sound of Mariam's dulcet voice than the sense of her words. At last she lowered her head and whispered, "Let us pray."

With her command, Tom fell into such a reverential state as he had not experienced since the earliest days of his church attendance. His mind seemed to be filled with the sounds of a celestial organ and the sight of ranks of cherubs and angels hovering amid golden clouds. If this had been what Nathan had undergone, Tom understood his swoon. He could barely hold onto consciousness himself.

After innumerable hours of almost orgiastic devotion, Tom suddenly sensed, in a vague way, that Mariam had risen from his side. In a second, she was back. Tom saw her pale hand enter his vision, bearing a goblet filled with white liquid.

"Drink now, my pilgrim," Mariam said.

Tom took the cup, and raised it to his lips.

A foul odor as of boiled worms filled his nostrils. The devotional haze was swept from his brain by the odor, and he began to gag. The cup fell from his hands and spilled *siqoqtoaq* across the black rug like a puddle of spoiled night-mare's milk.

Tom stood angrily, rage making him master of himself again. "What were you doing?" he forced between clenched teeth. Had any of the foul drug passed his lips?

Mariam seemed incontrite. "You were almost ready," she declared. "Your soul was prepared to accept the glory of Saint Fiune and his God."

"How can you say that? You can't see my soul."

"Oh, but I could. It floated beside mine, amidst the heavenly choir."

Tom regarded Mariam dubiously. Having escaped the draught of *siqoqtoaq*, he began to calm down. The girl was obviously as deluded as the rest of the inhabitants of the Black Demesne, and Tom's protests would never change her mind. In the end, he said only, "You misread the condition of my soul."

"'Tis no matter," Mariam graciously replied. "Perhaps when you witness the Test, you will be convinced to take the holy potion."

"What is this Test you all keep referring to?" Tom asked, grateful to speak of something else.

"Whenever we move up to a new floor, closer to Heaven, we must ascertain if we have finally reached those heavenly heights where the body is freed from all earthly gravity. This we accomplish by permitting one of the holiest among us to jump from the new level."

Tom shuddered, picturing the long drop.

At that moment a monk entered. "All are gathered for the Test, Sister Mariam. The Patriarch has decreed that the devout pilgrim who kissed his feet shall be the lucky participant."

"What?" shouted Tom. He pushed past the monk, out into the corridor.

There, at the end with the door opening onto the frigid sky, stood a group of people, the Patriarch instantly recognizable among them by his white locks.

"Natty! Lug!" Tom yelled. "Come quick!"

Without waiting to see if they responded, Tom began to run, feet pounding the black tiled floor. The sacrificial group appeared so intent as not to heed his noisy approach.

Tom burst through the outer ranks of the gathered monks. There he saw a horrifying scene.

Nathan stood with a blank face at the brink of the drop. In his embrace was Lug, whose arm and foot were doubled up and bound with rope. Apparently, tossing out this ungodly creature was planned to add luster to the sacrifice.

"Prepare thy soul," the Patriarch intoned. "Be pure of heart, and you will ascend."

"Yes," mumbled Nathan. "Ascend . . ."

Natty ran up behind Tom, breaking Tom's trance.

"No!" Tom shouted. He bulled through the crowd and grabbed Nathan's cape. With a yank, he pulled the preacher away from the edge and pushed him back amid the monks, where Natty took charge of him and Lug.

The Patriarch stood close by Tom, shaking with barely suppressed rage like an oak in a storm. "What doth this mean?" he finally thundered out.

A myriad, myriad pieces of a gigantic, deeply consequential puzzle fell into place within Tom's mind when the Patriarch spoke.

Without thinking, Tom reached up and grasped the Patriarch's beard and tresses.

Then he ripped them off.

The Bastard King himself stood revealed. His bald, contorted pate suffused with blood, and his face split with hatred.

"*Arrgh!*" he bellowed.

A savage shove from his antagonist's meaty hands sent Tom reeling out the door into the heavens.

The last thing Tom saw was two small clawed lizard paws poking from the Patriarch/King's mouth.

Still clutching the wig and false beard, Tom fell. The icy wind whistled around his plummeting body as he screamed:

"Mab!"

9
Vision, Trial and Entrance

> "For from the air above, and the grassy
>   ground beneath,
> "And from the mountain-ashes and the old
>   White thorn between,
> "A Power of faint enchantment doth through
>   their beings breathe,
> "And they sink down together on the green."
>   — Sir Samuel Ferguson, "The Fairy Thorn"

Tom was a child again, and his mother was rocking him to sleep for his afternoon nap. A temperate breeze played over his face, teasing at his closed lids. The suggestion of gentle sunlight also beckoned him to toss off his drowsiness and clamber out of his cradle. *There is so much to see and do in the world*, the air and the light seemed to say. *You are young, cast off your slumber. Rise up and explore.*

Exploration was so much work, though, thought Tom drowsily. Sleep was lovely. Sleep held no real dangers. There were no decisions to be made in sleep, no choices between good and evil. One merely flowed with what happened, a dreamer adrift in the coracle of his own subconscious.

The rocking continued. Why should he fight his mother's ministrations? He *was* tired, so very tired, he realized now. Let sleep wash over him forever . . .

"Tom," said a woman's voice. "Tom, it's time to wake up. You've slept long enough."

Was that his mother calling? It didn't sound like her. Whoever it was, why couldn't she make up her mind? First she rocked him, then she shocked him. Which was it to be? To sleep or to wake, that was the question . . .

"Tom," the woman called. "Please, Tom — wake up!"

She sounded nice.

On such a slim basis, Tom chose consciousness, and all it implied.

He opened his eyes upon Mab's face. She wore her concern and worry more beautifully than most women wore happiness. Her grey eyes brimmed with tears which she seemed to refuse to shed by simple strength of will. The downturned corners of her silver-glossed lips tugged at the nets of tiny wrinkles that sought to anchor them in this unaccustomed position. Tom noticed that her long platinum hair was bound with a fillet of the same color, set with a moonstone that gleamed in the center of her brow.

Seeing Tom wake, Mab quickly changed. As if her heart could hold no scars, or her memory no impress, from events that were past and beyond changing, her expression reverted instantly to that fey combination of humor and solemnity, low urges and high purposes, which had enchanted Tom from the instant he came upon her, as she lay reading on the fernie brae.

"Well and good," Mab said. "You've made up your mind to rejoin us. I can't do everything for you, you know. If you had determined to leave us now, to give in to the airy chill of the Black Demesne and drift off into an endless doze, I would have been powerless to call you back."

Tom sat up. Beneath him was a soft bed of white silks and pillows. Gauzy curtains and a canopy of green shielded him on three sides and above. The whole platform beneath him continued to roll slowly from side to side.

Mab's words held implicit information on a topic Tom couldn't quite fasten on at first. But then concerns came to him like lightning.

"Us!" he said. "My comrades! Natty, Lug, Nathan — where are they? Are they okay? Did they get back from the Tower? Mab, it was awful. You don't know —"

"But I do know," Mab contradicted. "I was watching all along through Lug's eyes. And I'm proud of you, Tom. You weren't speaking idly, back at the Fork, when you said you would recognize anywhere what you had once seen."

Tom recalled the sourceless inspiration that had caused him to snatch off the Patriarch/King's disguise. What that charade meant, he still wasn't sure. Perhaps if he could talk with Mab about it —

Mab diverted Tom with a wave of her hand. No charm this, but merely a summons to a trio of offstage shadows lurking beyond the flimsy cloth wall.

A blue meteor landed on the bed beside Tom and began pummeling him on the back. Lug's ugly face seemed nearly bisected by his big-toothed smile.

Crowding around the bed were Nathan and Natty. The red-haired dandy was ebullient and somehow self-congratulatory in his motions, as if shouldering all the credit for having gotten them out of the Black Demesne. He pumped Tom's hand while peppering him with a barrage of adjectives that might have applied equally to Tom's recovery, the weather, or Natty's own superb digestive abilities.

"Excellent! Marvelous! Most satisfactory!"

Nathan, meanwhile, was perhaps more morose than usual, if such a state were possible. He gripped Tom's free hand in both of his, and beseeched him with a hangdog look. The minister's bass lamentations seemed wrenched from the roots of his heart.

"Thomas, lad, I beg your forgiveness. Had I but sackcloth and ashes, I would don them — and a hairshirt too. I cannot explain, nor can I ever condone, my misguided spontaneous conversion to the faith of those obscene wheel-wearers. I was transported entirely out of myself — no doubt much as Job was when he cursed God. But I have learned my lesson. The Lord wants no such abject adoration from his true followers, or abandonment of wholesome society. My old course has been confirmed to me as the right one. I shall endeavor by doing good to repay any discomfort I might have caused you, Lug, and this foppish reprobate beside me."

Tom tried to say that Nathan shouldn't worry, but the cheerful violence of his friends, and their questions and exclamations, did not permit him to get a word out.

After a few minutes of watching this treatment with a sly smile, Mab said, "All right, gentlemen, Lug — leave Tom alone now. He's still exhausted and hungry, whereas you three have all eaten. Let him get up, and come to table."

Tom's three companions ceased their various greetings and helped him to stand. On unsteady feet, he left Mab's tent.

Outside, he found himself on a sizable swan-shaped boat floating at anchor in the middle of a wide, cerulean loch. A few feet away, a silver mast pierced the blue sky, white sails snapping softly upon it. Mab's vessel rocked on the gentle catspaws ruffling the waters.

A table was set back in the stern, behind the fabric cabin. Tom eyed the feast spread there with a sudden knot of hunger clenching his stomach.

"You three may rest in the bow," said Mab, "while

Tom and I eat. Tom and I have much of a private nature to discuss."

Reluctantly, as if fearful of being separated again, Tom's friends moved off toward the graceful neck of the swan-boat, where there awaited cushions and refreshments (could that be beer, for Natty, which Tom though he whiffed?).

Mab conducted Tom back to the table, and they sat on low, three-legged stools.

On a cloth of white linen were dozens of dishes. Same held cooked vegetables — potatoes, carrots, turnips — while others held, of course, fruit. And thick slices of wheat bread were already smeared with creamy butter. But the centerpiece of the banquet was a large platter on which lay a spotless golden trout, brassy as hammered sunlight and garnished with parsley. Its skin bore no sear-marks of grill or oven, yet from it wafted a delectable odor of cooked flesh.

Tom didn't know what to attack first. His stomach seemed as empty as if he had not eaten since setting out upon the black Road. He compromised by grabbing two pieces of bread, inserting a slab of cheese, and eating the sandwich between bites from an apple.

"Let me serve you some fish," said Mab. With a three-tined fork and long knife, she severed the fish's head. Its uppermost milky eye seemed to fix on her imploringly. She sliced a good-sized portion of the fish's body and placed it on a silver plate in front of Tom.

Tom tasted the fish. Its flaky flesh was improbably

sweet, like nothing he had ever experienced before, It seemed to gently diffuse within his mouth, dissolving without chewing. Tom swallowed his first mouthful heartily, and then, careful of bones, disposed of the rest of his portion. Mab served him again, and he ate the second piece as greedily as the first. Each bite of the fish seemed to stoke his appetite for more.

Before he knew it, the whole fish had been reduced to translucent bones, a scaly tail and the eyeless head. The golden trout seemed to have imbued Tom with a knowledge he could not put into words. His mind felt keen and capable of dazzling flights of logic, illogic and metalogic. He turned to Mab, eager now to discuss all he had seen.

Mab seemed disposed to banter first. "Did you enjoy the trout?" she asked.

"Yes," Tom said. "Very much. I've never seen one that color, or tasted its like."

"Nor shall you ever again. There was only one such fish in all of Faerie."

"Oh, really?" Tom asked with interest, hoping to learn more about Mab's realm at last, now that he had been through so much at the Queen's bidding.

"Indeed," said Mab, steadily regarding Tom. "He was my late husband."

Tom stared at Mab. Her lips were straight as a ruler. Did they flicker slightly as Tom watched? Did her grey eyes dance? Tom couldn't be sure.

"You're joking," he said.

Mab was silent.

"You're telling the truth," he tried.

Mab nodded.

Tom stood and went to lean over the carved tail of the swan. He tried to feel sick, but couldn't. He felt wonderful, invigorated, and wasn't able to shake the bliss. So he gave up trying, and returned to Mab.

"We have a place to go to, Tom," Mab said. "We only dallied here since I thought these waters a congenial spot for you to return to, after the rigors of the Patriarch's court. But now I'll set us in motion, and we can talk as we travel."

With her words, the boat began to move in a straight line across the loch — whatever anchoring force there had been, now released.

Tom, still struggling with the revelation of what — who? — his meal had been, tried to order his thoughts into the many questions he had for Mab.

Unwittingly or purposefully, she provided the springboard for their dialogue.

"I am afraid that your scrip and staff got left behind, in the Tower."

For the wallet, Tom felt only a brief pang. Lent by his Uncle Ross, filled with relatively new things, it did not mean as much as the short staff. An image of his well-worn, cherished stick — the last thing saved from his prior life, now that Master Alighieri's book had been destroyed — welled up in Tom with almost unbearable poignance. How, he wondered, could such a simple thing carry so enormous a freight of meaning? It was only a length of hawthorn, marked with miles and memories. Well, it was gone now, perhaps to fire the kilns that baked the black bricks. To mourn it would be foolish.

Tom turned to more important matters. He said the only thing he was certain of, in a cautious way:

"The King and the Patriarch, Mab — they were one and the same man. And there wasn't a groat's worth of difference between their two lands. Why, even both their grandiose schemes had the same flaw. The Tower and the Pit were going to dwindle to points long before they reached their goals."

Mab nodded.

"And that legend Mariam told me," Tom went on tentatively, "the one about the two leaders meeting and initiating Armageddon. How can they meet if they're the same person?"

"Obviously," said Mab, "they never can."

"Does that mean that the world will never end, then, as the Bible foretells?"

"No, Tom, it never will. At least not for a longer span of time than you can ever conceive of. And when it does end, it will be not with a bang, but a whimper. And until that distant hour, good and evil will continue, just as you witnessed them."

Tom began to fume. "I can't believe that. Won't the Patriarch's court revolt, now that I've unmasked him?"

"Certainly not, Tom," Mab replied calmly. "It will all be rationalized somehow. They'll say you were a demon sent to test their faith, the Patriarch will fashion a new hairpiece, and everyone will go right back to believing what they always did."

"Damn it!" said Tom. "It's all a huge charade. Can't anyone see through it?"

"You ask too much of people, Tom. You ask them to abandon cherished illusions — perhaps the only things that enable them to survive — for an unpalatable truth. People need to believe in opposites to keep going on with their lives. How else could they ever know what to strive for, or avoid? They certainly won't think for themselves. No, the truth is not for everyone, Tom. Only certain souls can accept it, or live with it."

Tom banged the table. "What's the truth in this case? I have to know! If evil is good, and good is evil, then which is real, which is primary?"

"Both," said Mab. "And neither."

"But I saw evil wearing a disguise in the kingdom of good. Does that mean that evil alone exists?"

"Think again, Tom," Mab urged. "Do you recall how I let our game of chess determine which branch of the Road you would first travel? An accident of chance dictated that I would play red, and my skill insured that I would win. Now — suppose I had played black, and won."

Tom thought, then ventured, "I would have visited the Black Demesne first."

"Correct."

"And then," he hesitantly continued, "when I went to the Scarlet Empire, I would have realized, I hope, that the Bastard King was merely the Patriarch without his hair."

"And then what would you have thought?"

Tom reluctantly said, "That conventional good was the only force, and was masquerading as conventional evil, for reasons I couldn't fathom."

Mab said nothing, but only inclined her beautiful chin slightly.

Words trembled upon Tom's tongue, a fateful revelation like a white hart, which, once loosed, could never be recalled. "Then the truth — the truth is just whatever's left after all your illusions are gone."

The deer bounded away, flicked its tail impudently, and vanished, leaving only the certainty of its having been.

"And Faerie," said Mab, "is truth. No illusions, Tom. Forever. That's how and where you and the world harmonize at last."

Tom stood without further speech and moved to the starboard rail. The breeze of the ship's majestic passage sent a faint chill up his spine. He put his hands up the wide sleeves of his tattered, borrowed shirt — donned amid such confusion in Shiverick's *Sanctum for Wayward Ladies* on a night so far removed from the present moment in time and space, experience and wisdom — and gripped his forearms tightly. What Tom now knew filled him with unsayable things he longed to say. Was this his fate, to be doomed to a silence composed of ineffable thoughts?

Mab came to stand behind him. "I know what is happening within you, Tom. It is something incompatible with this mortal world. Take my word for it: things will be better when you get where we're going."

Tom turned to Mab, wishing he could hate her for doing this to him. "And where is that?"

"Back to the Fork."

"What's there?" Tom demanded. "What's left for me there? I've been down both Roads."

"Every Fork has three tines, Tom," was all Mab would say, before retreating to her tent and dropping the flap.

Tom went forward to his friends. Natty greeted him with an effusive burp. Lug seemed several sheets to the wind also, empty flagons smelling of hops and malt at his foot. And Nathan appeared still distracted by thoughts of what had happened to him in the Black Demesne, making him unfit for conversation.

It was just as well, for Tom didn't know what he would have said.

The men and fachan idled in the bow for several hours, as the ship journeyed on. The loch had emptied into a broad river which carried them through forest and plain. Eventually the current faltered — although the ship continued apace, even without a wind — and the river spread out into a marshy delta.

After further hours, when the marsh became too shallow for the swan-ship's draft, and the channels too narrow for her breadth, there came a change in locomotion. Suddenly the ship rose up on six slender legs and began to scuttle smoothly through the swampy terrain.

Tom felt a brief startlement at this development, then soon sank back into his wordless musings.

At last appeared a paved tumulus like a hard-backed snake: the Great Road as raised up by its anonymous ancient builders in order to carry it over the lowlands.

The swan-boat gained the checkered surface of the Road and continued toward the Fork, swiftly retracing the weary way Tom and the others had once walked, after Nathan and Natty had joined the party.

Shortly they reached the spot where the Road split.

Looking straight ahead, into that morass between the arms of the Y, which had seemed so insubstantial on two previous occasions, Tom thought to see — but no, it couldn't be. He knuckled his eyes in disbelief.

Mab had left her tent. At her wordless command, the ship retracted its legs and settled on the pavement. A section of rail vanished and a silver gangplank tongued out. Mab walked down, and the others followed.

They stood for the third time where two paths diverged.

"Natty, Nathan," said Mab. "I must ask now what you plan to do. You cannot accompany Tom any further."

Although Tom had suspected that this moment was coming, it still hurt to realize that it was here. To lose these two familiar comrades, who had accompanied him

through all his turbulent adventures — it was an almost
insupportable blow.

Rushing to speak and cover his agitation, Tom said,
"Perhaps you two will return to Ercildoune. Yes, I'm
sure that's the town for you."

Natty eyed Nathan, and the preacher returned his
glance. They seemed to be recalling the separate commit-
tees that had escorted both of them out of town the last
time.

"No," said Natty. "I think I can speak for old Silverprick here when I say that such a move would not be to
our best advantage."

"Well," said Tom, singling out his carrot-haired
friend, yet reluctant to say what he dreaded, "I guess
you'll be going back to the Scarlet Empire, Natty. Lilith
will be sure to give you an exciting reception, and you
seemed quite at home there."

Natty shook his head in the negative. "That would
have been my very intention not long ago, Tom, my
lad. But I've been doing a bit of thinking since then. It
seems like too much of a good thing in that bloody
land, if you take my meaning. Say I could fit in, and
could gratify all my, ahem, basest desires by lifting a
finger. Well, where's the challenge in that? No, I have
something else in mind. That last place we visited —
those folks seem never to have heard of cards or gaming
or wenching. That little piece of pious tail sitting
at the Patriarch's feet represents quite a conquest,
could one ever heat her up. So I think, if it's all

right with you, that I'll be heading down the black Road."

Natty looked off down that very branch, rubbing his hands together in anticipation.

Tom was taken completely aback. All he could think to say was :

"I — I wish you and Nathan good luck then in the Tower of the Patriarch. Watch out for each other."

Nathan spoke up. "What do you mean, son? I'm not going back to that damnable place where I nearly lost my life."

Tom sputtered. "But I thought — That is —"

"No, Tom," said the black-caped preacher, "don't try to dissuade me. My mind's made up, with the force of revelation. Can you forget those swarming trolls and the misery they lived in, back in the Scarlet Empire? Why, think of poor Gorget's widow, with all those mouths to feed, and perhaps even another litter on the way, what with the way those two were enjoying themselves that night. Yes, I heard it too, and almost interrupted their coupling with admonitions on concupiscence. Now I'm glad I didn't, since it was the last pleasure poor Gorget had. The way I interpret the sacred text, the least little improvement I can make in the lives of those benighted trolls will shine in the eye of the Lord like a beam of heavenly light."

Tom felt overwhelmed. He didn't know what to say.

So he said nothing, but only fell upon Nathan and Natty, hugging them fiercely. They returned his embrace. And when Lug joined in one-armedly, Tom began to cry.

At last they broke apart. Mab, who had been silent, said, "My blessings on both of you men. Having aided Tom staunchly, you deserve my thanks. And you have both chosen more wisely than most. It is always better to test oneself against a powerful foe than to slothfully follow the line of least resistance. Before you go, heed my words: the two branches of the Road — which you have never traversed all the way — having been separately diverted, curve and rejoin again. Pass through all that awaits you, and you may meet again, on the far side of good and evil. Go now, with glad hearts."

Natty and Nathan, having absorbed Mab's words, separated now, each setting foot upon their individual Road.

"So long, Tom," said Natty. "And you too, Shiverick. We'll compare notes someday soon, where the Roads rejoin."

"Mend your ways, Master Spurgeon," said Nathan, "so that I can travel with you in the future without doing violence to my principles. And fare thee well, Tom."

The two men strode off, waving back for some distance. Tom, still tearful, swivelled his head from one to the other, until he lost sight of them both.

Turning to Mab, wiping a few stray tears from his eyes, Tom said, "They'll never change, will they, Mab?"

"Not in any real way," Mab replied, "although most humans still surprise me by how much they can improve.

But your two friends are too perfectly what they are. And that's why they could not come where we're going."

Tom did not ask the name of their destination, for he knew it must be Faerie. How they were to reach it from this desolate, unlikely place — whose possibilities he believed he had fully explored — was what puzzled him. He was about to ask Mab to explain this very matter, when she shocked him once more.

"Tom," the Queen of Faerie said, "before we leave this mortal earth, I am ready to grant you whatever remains on this human globe that your heart most desires."

Tom had thought that nothing else could take him by surprise. He had seen so much, and had so many cherished beliefs shattered, that he had felt ready to accept anything that came his way. At this point in his life, he thought, nothing should strike him as improbable or unlikely. When he had rid himself of one particular illusion — the flimsy veil masking the true face of good and evil — he had thought that he understood everything. But now, hearing Mab's impossible offer, he realized that he understood very little, that many, many more veils — perhaps a lifetime's worth — remained before his eyes. He had barely completed his first step on the infinitely long road to truth — taking truth as he himself had so tentatively defined it: whatever was left after all illusions were gone. The paramount falsehood to destroy, he suddenly realized, was the illusion that he had no more illusions.

A sudden wave of fatigue and despair washed over Tom. All the subtle wit and bodily energy that he had derived from his meal of golden trout seemed to have deserted him. He felt himself to be simply a very young man who had barely begun an incredibly long journey which had already sorely tried him. He pictured what he must look like. Begrimed and bewhiskered, save for his Mab-given bald patch on his jaw; accoutered in the rags of some stranger; sunken-cheeked, heat-blasted and frost-bitten from exertions in two mad empires; bereft of all tokens such as book and stick that had once meant home to him — This mental image filled him with further dismay.

How, in this state, could he even begin to imagine what he most desired in the familiar earth?

Something that had just crossed his mind recurred with haunting significance. Home — That was it. He wanted to go home. Not to stay permanently, striving to forget all he had learned, becoming a sour and crabbed soul, who would feel he had wasted his one chance in life. And not to the community of his birth as it currently existed, to dwell with Uncle Ross raising turnips for the rest of his life. No, Tom had known such an existence was not for him even before setting out upon the Great Road. The home he wanted to return to for just a final glimpse didn't exist anymore, except in the past. By any rational stretch of the imagination, it must be inaccessible, forever out of reach. He shouldn't get his hopes up.

Yet what had been rational about the events that had

happened to him? And would Mab have offered any-thing imaginable if she couldn't come through?

Tom probed around the matter, as one approaches a sore tooth with inquisitive tongue.

"You once told me that there were no dichotomies in Faerie. Does that apply to time?"

For a full minute, Mab studied Tom intently, with a look that seemed to say: *Be very careful, my friend, and consider what you ask!*

"Time," she replied at last, "is a curious thing in Faerie. In one respect, it is as inexorable as here on earth. Time took my husband from me as surely as if he had dwelt among men. But then again, he was only a mortal, and yet he still lived centuries in Faerie.

"On the other hand, time does not wear the three separate masks in Faerie which it dons on earth. Time past, time present, time future — all are one in my land, in a strange way that diminishes none of their individuality."

Tom made up his mind. "Then I know what I want. Take me back, if you can, to that night when my home was raided, and my life changed so much. Take me back to that last night when I was my old self."

A soft sigh escaped Mab's pearly lips, as if something she had foreseen but was helpless to alter had come true.

"Done," she said.

A breath carried them from day to night, and over leagues of land.

Dark clouds scudded in the moonless sky, and whis-

tling winds bent the limbs of the trees surrounding the
clearing wherein stood Tom's cottage. The April air was
heavy with humidity, auguring the rains to come. A rich
medley of smells permeated the clearing, filling Tom's
nostrils with a heady scent he knew with unmistakable
force: the unique blend of rotting leaves and fallen
branches, of growing plants and hidden fungi, of sleeping sheep and corn cradled in its crib, all of which added
up to home.

Beside Tom stood Mab and Lug. He barely noticed
them, so enrapt was he with the full force of his impossible homecoming. His mind kept trying to superimpose
visions of a smoldering pile of coals atop the humble,
happy croft just a few yards away. Yet the reality of this
as-yet undamaged night was too palpable, too undeni-
able, to admit the future disaster. Tom had a sudden sense
of this moment as an eternal thing, solid and imperishable
as a diamond, which nothing could ever alter or erase.
Future events had no dominion here. What was at this
moment was forever, and could not be diminished. He
knew his old self — so much younger in experience and
knowledge, so much happier in a primitive way! — now
sat within the little cottage, from whose shuttered windows wriggled thin worms of candlelight. He knew his
mother was there, knitting a garment that would never be
finished. He knew they had been and would be there forever, despite whatever happened next.

"Stay here," Tom said to Mab and Lug, in a trance-
bound voice. "I must see them."

He walked slowly across the cleared ground, heedless of roots or stones, his autonomous feet treading the well-known path to his front door.

After what seemed almost as long a journey as all the weary way he had travelled since this very night, Tom found himself on the foot-polished flat stone that served as their front step. Raising one hand, he knocked upon his door.

From within, the faint sound of clicking needles stopped. As if the door did not exist, Tom could see what was happening inside. His mother had laid down her knitting in her lap, and the younger Tom — who both was and was not the same person as the Tom who stood outside — had closed his book with forefinger caught between the pages. Tom longed to hear their voices once more, although he knew their conversation by heart. But thunder suddenly resounded, and the hum of their speech was drowned out.

Give him time, thought Tom. Time to finish speaking, to stand, to set book down on chair, to go to the door, to grasp the stick as protection — and now!

Outside, Tom knocked a second time.

The pin securing the door rattled briefly, as it left its hasp. An unoiled hinge gave a slight *creak*. The fire inside snapped, and Tom gave a slight jump, in sympathy with his interior twin. Recovering, he knocked —

— for the third and final time.

The mass of broad planks swung reluctantly open. Tom, standing like a thief in the night, was grateful that the door, opening inward and to his right, would block his mother's view of their late-night visitor. He knew she wouldn't understand what he had become.

Tom saw his youthful double before his double's light-accustomed eyes saw him. Light streamed out over young Tom's shoulders, leaving his face in shadow. He wore the comfortable homespun clothes Tom had lost ages ago. Even in the semi-darkness, young Tom's full face seemed embarrassingly unformed and immature. Why was he standing there like such an idiot? Why didn't he speak? Tom wasn't about to hurt him. He just wanted to — to what? Say hello? Clasp his hand? Tell him what to watch out for? Suddenly, he couldn't figure out why he had even come back.

Lightning cracked the heavens then, a hieroglyph that Tom could read all too well.

As fast as I travel, the lightning spelled out, *so fast does a life change forever.*

In the unnaturally prolonged moment during which the lightning hung like a signboard in the sky, Tom studied his earlier self. What a goose he was! Mab had been right to so name him, when he prostrated himself before her at their first meeting. He wanted to grab his young self and shake some sense into him. But he knew it was impossible.

The lightning died. Young Tom shouted and stumbled back. Thunder called. A second bolt of fire answered across the night.

Tom saw a look of utter fear pass over the face of the boy in the doorway. What could have caused — Tom suddenly remembered.

He looked down and to his side. Lug stood there, grinning in what was surely a friendly way, but which those unacquainted with the fachan might possibly mistake for bloodthirsty anticipation.

"Damn it all, Lug!" Tom yelled. "I told you to stay back! Now you've spoiled everything!"

At that instant, the second flash of lightning returned to nothingness, the door was slammed in Tom's face, and Lug hopped away.

Tom knew there was no point in remaining upon the step. His younger self would not return. Already, the boy's racing heart was slowing behind the door, and he was telling his mother only half the truth about who had appeared. Soon, he would begin puttering about the cottage prior to sleep, picking up a mug, placing his book upon its shelf and walking stick by the door, where he could grab both items later, when the raiders came. And winding the clock. Oh yes, Tom thought with a silent, ironic laugh, he would be sure to wind the clock, believing that time could be so easily controlled.

Tom stepped away from his cottage for the last time.

Now all he wanted to do was find Mab and Lug and return to the Fork.

His knowledgeable feet took him again across the clearing, to the path that lead out to the Great Road. The wind was rising, an occasional droplet striking Tom's brow. He didn't want to hang around for what he knew must happen. Where was Mab?

Tom began softly to call her name. Surely she couldn't have taken to the woods. If anywhere, she must be a little ways down the path, keeping circumspectly back from his reunion with himself.

Heading down the trail, Tom called, "Mab? Where are you, Mab? I'm ready to go now."

There was no answer. Lug was nowhere to be seen either.

Tom continued down the path, not knowing what else to do. He had no guarantee that Mab had gone in this direction. But he had certain knowledge of what was going to happen in the clearing. So he kept walking away from it.

After an hour or so — just think of his younger self sleeping so peacefully in his cabinet-bed! — Tom came out upon the Great Road, here its triple self, rut, grass, and rut. Tom felt the pull of the Road beneath his shoes, impelling him toward the Fork. Would he have to walk all the way back there now, and wait for Mab to show up? But hold on a second — there had not been any version of Tom waiting at the Fork the first time he arrived. Did that mean he could not cause such a thing to occur, since it had not happened the first time? Tom's head ached with the speculation.

The whole matter was too paradoxical.

Deciding to avoid any possibility of creating such a

situation, Tom turned in the other direction, away from Ercildoune and the Fork.

He walked another mile or so, head down, mind busy with the implications of all that had happened to him, feet dragging. Around him, the storm gathered, threatening to break.

Then he saw Mab.

She stood in the center of the Road, her gown whipping about her in the wind, her silver hair blowing back. Her arms were raised up to the sky, her face — lit by a lightning flash — was wreathed with concentration. The moonstone set in her fillet glowed like a star.

Mab swept her arms down.

The Road filled with mounted men carrying scarlet-flamed torches. The landscape blazed with a familiar hellish radiance.

The horde of men and horses was silent and still, as their leader cantered forth to meet Mab.

"What do you want with me, Witch?" the Bastard King growled. "Have you not plagued me enough for centuries now, without demanding more?"

"Quiet!" said Mab. "I need you again, to fulfill what must be. There lies a croft not far from here, down the first path off the Road. Go to it, and do what you will."

Without further speech, the King reined his giant steed around, and waved his men into a gallop.

Standing in the Road, Tom couldn't believe what he had heard. He wanted to toss himself at Mab, at the thundering war-party, to stop them or die in the attempt.

But at the last moment before he was trampled flat, his traitorous body reacted instinctively to hurl himself out of their path.

When he stood, Mab was gone.

"Mab!" shouted Tom. "You bitch! Come back here and fight like a man!"

If she heard, Mab declined the challenge.

It had begun to drizzle. Tom punched the wet bark of a tree until his hand pained him. Then he went looking for Mab.

The hours passed in a roaring confusion of wind and rain and betrayal. Tom crashed through woods and splashed across streams, somehow having lost the Road. He cursed the sky and elements, the ground and his own foolish self, like the mad old king, Leir, in the folktale. Lightning smote the sky again and again, and rain soaked his clothing.

He found himself — after hours of wandering back and forth across bog and heath — back on the Great Road, at the same point he had left it.

Exhausted, he crouched by the roadside,.

Many hooves sounded in the distance, coming closer.

The Bastard King and his troops were returning to she who had summoned them.

Mab reappeared.

Tom was too tired to accost her.

One by one, as the riders approached Mab and passed through an invisible curtain, they were transformed.

Entering the point red, they emerged black and

pumpkin-headed. Last to enter, the Bastard King became the Patriarch.

The horde stopped and wheeled around, the Patriarch confronting Mab.

"Aroint thee, Succubus!" the Patriarch commanded. "Get thee from my sight!"

"It's you who shall leave, Patriarch. I bid you follow the tracks of your foe, the Bastard King, written here in the Road, and succor those whom he has wronged, in your own harsh fashion."

Pivoting, the Patriarch and his followers rode off posthaste, eager to do good.

Tom stood with a weariness that extended from scalp to feet. He approached Mab.

"Mab —" he began.

"Shush," said Mab. "Till this affair entire is over, I cannot take time to speak with you."

Resigned, indifferent, enervated, Tom sat in the muddy Road. When the rain became a torrent, he didn't even move. For the second time in his life, the same storm drenched him, giving lie to the ancient Greek who had claimed no man could step in the same river twice.

The Patriarch and his men returned. As they galloped into the unseen magical curtain of Mab's devising, they disappeared.

The world was silent save for the downpour.

Tom opened his mouth and —

— sunlight blinding him, said, "Mab."

They were back at the Fork. It was late afternoon,

almost sundown. Lug stood with them. Somehow he and Mab had remained undampened by the rains of days gone by.

"Why, Mab?" Tom continued, almost inured to such abrupt transitions in space and time. "Why did you do it?"

Mab's face registered neither anger nor remorse, disapproval nor approbation. Choosing her words with great deliberation, she asked, "Why did you chose to go back, Tom?"

Tom thought. "I — I couldn't help myself. It was what I most wanted."

"Whether you believe it or not, Tom," Mab said earnestly, "I could not help myself either. Once I stood back in the past with you, I realized that it was I who had first brought those twin plagues down upon your home. There was no other way they could have gotten there that night. I was powerless not to summon them, if I was to have you, and if you were to be worth having. But what was the ultimate cause for what you just witnessed? Was it my decision to offer you your heart's desire? Or was it your response, asking to return to the past? Can we even separate cause from effect in such a case as this?"

Pondering Mab's questions, Tom found no answer, but only another question. "Couldn't you have changed the past though, Mab, once you knew the truth? Couldn't you have foregone bringing King and Patriarch back to wreck my life?"

Mab seemed hurt, for the first time since Tom had

known her. "Maybe I could have, Tom. But I had desires of my own to satisfy. I wanted — still want you for my own. And initiating the chain of events that you experienced was the only way of getting you." She paused. "Have I really wrecked your life?"

Tom considered. Honestly, he said, "No, Mab. No, I guess you haven't done anything to me I didn't ask for."

Silence hung for a strained moment between them. Then Tom spoke:

"About wanting me, Mab — Why me, and for what?"

"For my husband, Tom. And as for why you — well, out of all mortals, why not you?"

Tom was utterly baffled. He would be Mab's mate? But that poor golden trout — What did it all mean?

"Look now, Tom," Mab said, and swept an arm up, directing his gaze toward the land that lay between the two arms of the Road.

The morass between the two Roads Tom had travelled, always so odd and insubstantial, was gone.

In its place was revealed the Road to Faerie, third tine of the Fork.

Verdant, flower-speckled meadows began just beyond the Road's cobbles and swept away to the horizon. The sky above this land was a dusky, rosy, purple-black, filled with stars and a full moon: perpetual twilight. His eyes swooping over each gentle moonlit vale and dell, Tom found himself drawn along the upward-sloping land to the last thing visible, before the curvature of the earth denied his eager gaze sight of further miracles.

A hill stood at the limits of his vision. Impossibly, if one rationally considered the distance involved, each blade of grass upon it was clear in his sight, as on that day when he had first met Mab. The hill was surmounted by two hawthorn trees, bearing white flowers. Their branches arched and met, so that they seemed to form a gate to all the wonders beyond.

"This is my realm, Tom," said Mab. "Since my last husband died — Tam Lin was his name — my domain has been cloaked in endless dusk, with moon and stars ascendent. Now, pleasant as I find the moon, it grows tiresome without the sun. Will you be my sun, Thomas?"

"Yes," said Tom, unable to tear his eyes away from the endless meadows that called to him with silent music.

"Then take these my tokens, Thomas."

Tom felt his wet clothing vanish, to be replaced by softer garments than any he had ever worn. Simultaneously, he found himself clutching something.

Looking down at himself, Tom saw he was arrayed all in green, like Mab. At his belt hung a set of panpipes. In one hand he held —

A harp. Gilded wood and silver strings, the instrument seemed molded to his grip, feeling as natural as his staff once had.

"I sense in your soul a bent for music, Thomas," Mab said. "After we get through this last trial, I'll find a teacher for you. Faerie boasts no end of fine musicians."

Tom raised his eyes from his splendid new suit. "'This last trial?'"

"A mortal's first entrance into Faerie is always hard," Mab replied. "But if you just hold tight to me, you'll be all right."

Tom nodded seriously, striving to imagine what there was left for him to endure.

Something wet and soft nuzzled his ear, and he jumped.

Thistle-bossed brasses rattled and mane-braided bells jingled.

Endymion stood foursquare behind him. He left off nibbling Tom's ear, tossed back his head and vented a tremendous horselaugh.

"Not now, Endymion," Mab sweetly admonished. "We have far to go before we rest and play. Come, Thomas, let Lug carry your harp, and mount up behind me."

Mab stirruped her foot and vaulted up. She lent a hand, and Tom followed suit.

Astride Endymion, Tom circled Mab's waist with his arms, remembering how he had once dared to try such a thing before, and been rebuffed. But now she only moved further into his embrace.

"Now, Lug, Endymion, Thomas — we're going home!"

Mab urged Endymion into a trot.

The horse's gold and silver hooves left the Road and bit the lawn, leaving a trail of crescents. Rich scents of loam and bruised grass filled the dusky air. They had set foot into Faerie, and left the mortal world of good and evil behind.

For a few minutes they moved through the elysian fields easily, their hair ruffled by a perfumed, halcyon breeze. Part of Tom wanted to glance backwards to witness one last time what he was forsaking. But at the same time, another part didn't care to. So he just held Mab the tighter, and looked in wonder about him, at the jewel-like flowers and shrubs.

Then he heard Endymion's hooves splashing in something. He looked down.

The grass was awash in sourceless blood thick as soup. Only the tips of the green blades still showed. The hot copper odor of it ascended to his nostrils, and drops of it, kicked up by the horse, splattered his pants. The bloody reflection of the moon and stars was a sickly parody of the heavenly display.

"Mab," Tom said, "I think there's something wrong."

"Hold tight, Thomas," was Mab's only reply.

Tom squeezed Mab until he wondered how she could breathe.

The blood was getting deeper. Soon it was up to Endymion's pasterns, and the horse had to lift each foot high out of the gruesome bath to advance. The sea of blood stretched away to left and right, and as far as Tom could see. Overhead, the sky had gone crimson, all trace of moon and stars vanished.

When the blood engulfed Tom's foot, he winced. It was hot, as hot as Lilith's hand. Surely it couldn't rise any further — could it?

"Mab, let's turn around," said Tom. "There must be an easier way to Faerie."

Mab said nothing.

When does a horse cease walking through a liquid and begin swimming? Tom believed it should have happened by now. The sticky blood was up to Tom's thighs, but still Endymion plodded on, refusing to float, his legs no longer even breaking the surface of the red sea.

The blood came up to Tom's waist —

— his chest —

— his chin.

"Mab," he gurgled, as it filled his mouth.

Still Endymion plowed on, through the scarlet flood.

Tom hadn't dared breathe or open his eyes since they had submerged. At last he could hold out no longer.

He took in a lungful of blood, opened his lids onto bloody visions.

The face of the Bastard King swam against a red backdrop, leering and laughing at him. Despite his fear and confusion, Tom longed to strike out at this tormentor. He raised one hand from Mab's waist, and felt a strong current in the bloody sea surge and threaten to tear him from his seat. Quickly he dropped his fist and clung again to Mab.

Next appeared Lilith, naked and supple as snake. She stroked her hips and breasts, offering herself to Tom. He felt drawn to her by urges older than Eve. His body, mind and soul seemed ready to tear apart from each other, and whirl away the ego that had been Thomas Rhymer into the void.

Burying his head in Mab's unseen shoulder, he wept salty tears that failed to dilute the sea.

Miles seemed to disappear beneath the steady tromping of Endymion's hooves. A roaring filled Tom's ears, as if the sea were angry with him. Tom felt steeped in blood, nauseous and weak, but knew that it was as far to return as it was to go on.

Blood drained from his ears like rain from gutters, and he felt his head emerging. Soon, eyes, nose and mouth were exposed. Quickly now the blood retreated, faster than it had climbed. The land of Faerie as he had seen it from the Fork came back, unmarked by the deluge — as were, ultimately, he and his companions.

Lug hopped gleefully beside the riders, holding Tom's harp, as if congratulating Tom on his endurance. Tom was about to speak, telling Mab the ride hadn't been so bad, when he saw where they were heading.

A grassy knoll reared up in front of them. In its side gaped the jagged mouth of a cavern. Mab was heading straight for it.

Tom tried directing Endymion away from the cavern-mouth. "Gie, Endymion! Haw!"

The horse ignored Tom, veering neither left nor right, and soon they were in the cavern.

Light died away behind them, and blackness fell like a solid mass. The cave was damp and cold, the air still and close.

This detour isn't unbearable, thought Tom with relief, as they rode through the chilly darkness. Nothing like that awful sea of blood.

But then he felt a trickle of soil slide down his collar.

The cave was collapsing.

More dirt fell, pebbles too, in a hard rain on his skull. The gritty downpour clattered on the floor of the cavern, and the horse's hooves crunched it.

"Faster, Endymion, faster!" yelled Tom. "We'll be buried alive!"

Why was Mab putting him through this? Tom frantically wondered. Could anything possibly be worth it?

More debris poured down from the roof, and without thinking, Tom turned his face up, as if to gauge their chances.

Shovelsful of soil fell on them, filling Tom's nostrils and mouth and eyes. The cave-in was fully underway now, and continued as they moved.

Soon Tom was completely entombed. Dirt gritted against his eyes and skin. He felt as if he had inhaled a whole cemetery. He hoped he would soon pass out and die.

But he didn't. Instead, he could feel that they actually

still moved, like moles or worms through the compacted earth, against enormous resistance.

Tom sensed that, despite the cloaking soil, he still clutched Mab. He squeezed her as hard as he could, knowing that if he let her go, the soil-friction would pull him off the horse.

Visions now belabored him. The hoary bust of the Patriarch appeared, damning Tom to an endless hell for profaning the Patriarchal person. Tom kept his arms around Mab. When Mariam materialized, kneeling and penitent, seeming to pray for Tom's soul, silently urging Tom to join her, Tom turned his face away, experiencing again that seductive bliss he had known when he knelt beside the holy sister.

Their progress was now a crawl. There seemed little difference between immobility and what Endymion so laboriously achieved with his mighty legs. The weight of the whole world sat on Tom's shoulders. His lungs felt as if they were full of rocks, and his mouth tasted like loam. The soil seemed a cocoon he would never shed.

When first his knees, and then his hands, felt open air, he couldn't believe it. The clinging mould seemed like his natural medium, so long had they been buried. In a second, Endymion, Mab, Tom and Lug burst fully from a hillside, which they yet left unmarred behind them.

Tom looked around, hardly daring to believe he had been reprieved from his premature burial.

They stood at the foot of the hill Tom had glimpsed

from so far away. At its crown stood the two hawthorn trees, clusters of snowy flowers nestled amid their glossy leaves. Stars glimmered through the interstices of flowers and foliage.

Tom, without asking if the trial were over, dropped down from Endymion. A second later, Mab had alighted beside him.

"Leave us now," Mab said to Endymion and Lug.

With shy backward glances, unlike any they had ever bestowed on Tom before, the horse and fachan did as ordered, Lug first returning to Tom the harp.

Mab took Tom's hand. "From here we go on foot."

Together, they climbed the grassy slope.

At the top, Tom looked back the way they had come.

Faerie stretched away endlessly, a shadowy, mysterious vista lit by stars and moon. There was no sign of his old world.

He turned back to Mab —

— who lay naked on a bed of crushed ferns, beneath the blossom-laden hawthorn boughs. Her aureoles and nipples were silver as her lips. Her pubic escutcheon was a nest of argent curls.

"True Thomas," she said.

And then his clothes were gone.

Epilogue

"That is a doubtful tale from Faery,
"Hard far the non-elect to understand."
— John Keats, "Lamia"

The man drops naked to his knees before his bare recumbent bride, upon the bonny bracken. He sees/will see/has always seen every last detail of his new land with a startling hyperacuity. A fallen cluster of hawthorn blossoms is a Milky Way in miniature, infinite as a universe. The grass around the man and woman's nuptial bed is a veritable forest filled with clambering beetles and ants, mantises and grasshoppers, all silvered by moonlight, who seemed to be gathering in a circle around the groom and bride. The bark of the hawthorns is crevassed deep with valleys. Overhead, arriving from all parts of Faerie, flitter moths and butterflies, gnats and midges, dragonflies and fat bumblebees.

Laying down his harp (which resounds plangently, although no one strokes its strings), the man looks with love upon the woman stretched out before him like a banquet. Every hair on her head and loins seems to sprout a tiny moon-colored flame at its tip, so she seems afire coldly, burning forever without being consumed. Her slate eyes linger on the man, then close, while her pearly lips contrarily part.

She opens her legs.

The man sees that her inner thighs are whiter than milk, the lips of her sex like the petals of a silver rose. From her mons wells up that flowery scent that seems to the man to be the breath of Faerie itself.

He is like iron hot from the forge, ready to be quenched by the bath of her body, emerging tempered and true. He moves between her legs —

— they merge —

— and begin to make the sun.

Moving in immemorial rhythms, her hands upon his body boldly, his hands stroking her more-than-mortal flesh, the man and woman rock, like a boat upon surging waters.

Now around them innumerable twittering gleeful creatures, as yet invisible, have gathered, to witness this ceremony. The man, in the midst of this ecstatic union, senses these watchers. He realizes that the woman sent away the two companions of the journey, horse and fachan, merely to spare him embarrassment initially. But now those two are back, however insubstantially, and the man feels their familiar personalities impinge upon his mind. A horselaugh, an excited burst of hopping — these mark their joy at the union. (The man senses other hoppers present too, and a corner of his busy mind is glad his friend is back with his tribe.)

The mottled face of the moon is watching the duo's horizontal dance, as are the crows and robins that have flocked in and perched on the hawthorn branches, where they chatter softly among themselves. Rabbits and mice, moles and voles, foxes and pheasants, badgers and cats, have all gathered around, to watch this mating that has been/is/will be going on till its inevitable end that never comes.

The man and woman are growing more frantic, tongues meeting and moving to lap neck and nipple, underarm and cheek. Suddenly there is a change.

Without his willing the swap, in another instant transition, the man is on his back, the woman astride him, riding him like a horse. Her hands grip the pommels of his knees, while his hands stirrup her feet. Faster and faster they enlarge each other's senses.

Until at last they climax.

The heavens are rearranged.

In the east appears a golden orb, sun-king returning to his nighted realm. The moon and stars pale before his brassy face, and begin to flee. For a moment, both sun and moon share the sky. Then the moon sinks into the west, glad of the chance to rest, knowing it still will reign nightly.

And as the woman sinks down at rest upon the shining man, her platinum hair overspreading his chest like molten metal, he hears music from that instrument beside them which he knows he will play/has always played, a lyrical voice joined shortly by accompaniment from others musical voices hidden in the air:

Harp and pipe and symphony.

THE END